The Boxcar Children Mysteries

D0564190

The Mystery in New York
The Gymnastics Mystery
The Poison Frog Mystery
The Mystery of the Empty Safe
The Home Run Mystery
The Great Bicycle Race Mystery
The Mystery of the Wild Ponies
The Mystery in the Computer Game
The Honeybee Mystery
The Mystery at the Crooked House
The Hockey Mystery
The Mystery of the Midnight Dog
The Mystery of the Screech Owl
The Summer Camp Mystery
The Copycat Mystery
The Haunted Clock Tower Mystery
The Mystery of the Tiger's Eye
The Disappearing Staircase Mystery
The Mystery on Blizzard Mountain
The Mystery of the Spider's Clue
The Candy Factory Mystery
The Mystery of the Mummy's Curse
The Mystery of the Star Ruby
The Stuffed Bear Mystery
The Mystery of Alligator Swamp
The Mystery at Skeleton Point
The Tattletale Mystery
The Comic Book Mystery
The Great Shark Mystery
The Ice Cream Mystery
The Midnight Mystery
The Mystery in the Fortune Cookie
The Black Widow Spider Mystery
The Radio Mystery
The Mystery of the Runaway Ghost
The Finders Keepers Mystery
The Mystery of the Haunted Boxcar
The Clue in the Corn Maze
The Ghost of the Chattering Bones
The Sword of the Silver Knight
The Game Store Mystery
The Mystery of the Orphan Train
The Vanishing Passenger

The Giant Yo-Yo Mystery
The Creature in Ogopogo Lake
The Rock 'n' Roll Mystery
The Secret of the Mask
The Seattle Puzzle
The Ghost in the First Row
The Box That Watch Found
A Horse Named Dragon
The Great Detective Race
The Ghost at the Drive-In Movie
The Mystery of the Traveling Tomatoes
The Spy Game
The Dog-Gone Mystery
The Vampire Mystery
Superstar Watch
The Spy in the Bleachers
The Amazing Mystery Show
The Pumpkin Head Mystery
The Cupcake Caper
The Clue in the Recycling Bin
Monkey Trouble
The Zombie Project
The Great Turkey Heist
The Garden Thief
The Boardwalk Mystery
The Mystery of the Fallen Treasure
The Return of the Graveyard Ghost
The Mystery of the Stolen Snowboard
The Mystery of the Wild West Bandit
The Mystery of the Grinning Gargoyle
The Mystery of the Soccer Snitch
The Mystery of the Missing Pop Idol
The Mystery of the Stolen Dinosaur Bones
The Mystery at the Calgary Stampede
The Sleepy Hollow Mystery

THE BOXCAR CHILDREN GHOST-HUNTING SPECIAL

Featuring

The Mystery of the Midnight Dog
1–112

The Ghost at the Drive-In Movie
113–225

The Return of the Graveyard Ghost
227–331

created by
GERTRUDE CHANDLER WARNER

Albert Whitman & Company
Chicago, Illinois

The Boxcar Children Ghost-Hunting Special
created by Gertrude Chandler Warner

Copyright © 2015 by Albert Whitman & Company
Published in 2015 by Albert Whitman & Company

ISBN 978-0-8075-2846-4

Printed in the United States of America
10 9 8 7 6 5 4 3 2 1 LB 20 19 18 17 16 15

Cover art copyright © by Tim Jessell
Interior illustrations by Hodges Soileau, Robert Papp, and Anthony VanArsdale

For more information about Albert Whitman & Company,
visit our web site at www.albertwhitman.com.

THE BOXCAR CHILDREN

THE MYSTERY OF THE MIDNIGHT DOG

Created by
GERTRUDE CHANDLER WARNER

Contents

CHAPTER 1

Kudzu and the Ghost Finders

"Look! It looks just like a dinosaur!" Six-year-old Benny Alden pointed out the window of the car.

Henry, Jessie, and Violet Alden looked where their younger brother was pointing, and Watch, their dog, sat up and put his paws on the edge of the window. Only Grandfather Alden didn't look, because he was driving.

"You're right, Benny," said Henry, who was fourteen. "It does look like a dinosaur."

"I *think* it's an old house that's falling

down," said Violet, who was ten.

"Or being mashed by all those green vines that are covering it," Jessie said, who was twelve and often acted motherly toward her younger sister and brother.

"Those green vines are everywhere!" Benny exclaimed. "What are they?"

"The vines are called kudzu," Grandfather Alden told him. "It's considered a weed in the South. People have to fight to keep it from covering everything. I've read it can grow up to four inches a day."

"A monster vine that eats everything," said Jessie.

Benny shivered and pretended to be afraid. He leaned over and said, "Watch, be careful! You don't want to get eaten by the monster vines!"

Watch, a small dog who acted as if he were much bigger, peered out the window and cocked his head. He wasn't sure what Benny was talking about, but he was ready to face it.

Henry, who was sitting in the front seat next to Grandfather, looked up from the map he held. "It looks like we're almost there," he announced. "According to the map, we're only about twelve miles from Elbow Bend, Alabama."

"We are?" Benny asked. "Good. I'm hot. And thirsty!" he said.

"Not hungry, too?" Henry teased Benny.

Benny thought about that for a moment. "Maybe," he said. "I could be hungry, too."

"Don't worry, Benny," Grandfather Alden said. "I'm sure Sally Wade will have a nice cold drink and something waiting for us to eat." Mrs. Sally Wade was an old friend of Grandfather's who had invited the Aldens to visit.

"Oh, good." Benny bounced a little on the seat with excitement. "Then the only other thing we'll need is a good mystery to solve. Let's ask Mrs. Wade if she has a mystery for us when we get there."

"We'll do that," Grandfather agreed. "Although it's a small town, Elbow Bend is famous for its fine old houses. It was one of the first settlements in the state. It's bound to have at least one haunted house."

"Not Mrs. Wade's house?" Benny asked, sounding half afraid and half hopeful.

"No, probably not the Wade house," Grandfather said, smiling.

Benny looked relieved. "Look out, ghosts, here we come!"

With Henry reading the directions, Grandfather had no trouble finding Mrs. Wade's house. Like many of the houses they passed, it was a big old house with a wide front porch. Mrs. Wade's house had a porch upstairs and down and was painted white with dark green shutters. An old oak tree draped with moss shaded the front yard. Flower beds bloomed along the front walk and around the house.

"It doesn't look haunted at all," Benny said. "None of the houses we've passed look haunted."

"Maybe that's a ghost!" said Jessie as the front door of the house opened and a small silver-haired woman stepped out. She shaded her eyes with her hands to see the Aldens better.

Grandfather laughed. "That's no ghost. That's Sally Wade."

Mrs. Wade waved at them. "Y'all are just in time for iced tea and cookies," she called. "Come on in."

Benny and Watch ran up the front walk, while the others followed more slowly.

As Benny got closer, Mrs. Wade smiled. Lines crinkled at the corners of her brown eyes. "I think you must be Benny," she said.

"You're right!" Benny cried. "How did you know? Did Grandfather tell you?"

Before Mrs. Wade could answer, he went on, "And this is Watch. And here comes Jessie — she's twelve — and Violet — she's ten. Henry's fourteen, and we don't know how old Watch is, because we found him. I'm not sure how old Grandfather is, either."

"Old enough," said Grandfather, smiling. He came up the steps and gave Mrs. Wade a hug.

"It's so good to see you, James," Mrs. Wade said. "It's been much too long."

Just then, the door opened and two girls of about eighteen or nineteen came out.

"Hi," said Benny. "Did you bring the cookies?"

The taller of the two girls, who wore her dark brown hair pulled back in a ponytail, said calmly, "Not yet. We'll help you bring your luggage in and show you your rooms first. I'm Kate Frances Wade. Mrs. Wade is my grandmother."

She motioned to the girl next to her, who had curly red hair and green eyes. "And this is Elaine Johnston. She's a real practical joker. You have to keep an eye on her!"

"Call me Lainey," the girl said with a warm smile.

"I'm Benny," Benny said. After everyone had been introduced, Kate Frances and Lainey helped the Aldens bring in their suitcases and showed them to their rooms.

Benny especially liked his room, which was across the hall from Henry's. It was small and fitted neatly under the sloping roof at the back of the house. It had a window with a window seat. Benny and Watch knelt on the pillow there and peered out the window. They saw a big backyard with a garden in it.

"It's nice, Watch. But no boxcar," Benny said.

"Boxcar?" asked Kate Frances, who had taken Benny to his room.

"We have a boxcar in our backyard in Greenfield," Benny explained. "We used to live in it when we were orphans."

"You did?" Kate Frances raised her eyebrows in surprise.

"Yes. Before Grandfather found us and we went to live with him," Benny said.

Henry had come into the room and he and Benny told the story of how the Aldens thought the grandfather they didn't know would be mean so they found the old boxcar in the woods and decided to live there.

"That's where we found Watch," Benny put in.

"Then Grandfather found us," Henry explained. "And we went to live with him."

"And he moved the boxcar. It's behind our house in Greenfield now so we can still

visit it whenever we want," Benny concluded.

"That's quite a story," Kate Frances said. "I'm sorry we don't have a boxcar of our own."

"If you had a ghost, it would be almost as good," Benny said hopefully.

"A ghost? Hmmm. Why don't we go have some tea and cookies," suggested Kate Frances.

They went back downstairs and found Grandfather, Jessie, Violet, and Lainey gathered on the porch. Benny spotted the plate of cookies and the pitcher of iced tea on the porch table.

Lainey poured him a glass of iced tea and he took a cookie and went to sit on the porch swing with Jessie.

"I was talking about our jobs at Elbow Bend State Park," Lainey told them. "Kate Frances and I are working there and staying with Mrs. Wade this summer. We just finished our first year at the state university."

Mrs. Wade pushed open the screen door

and came out with a bowl of water, which she put in the corner of the porch in the shade. "For you, Watch," she said.

Mrs. Wade sat down. Kate Frances poured her some iced tea and said, "Benny's been telling me that he wishes we lived in a haunted house."

"Benny!" said Jessie.

"Well, maybe *next door* to a haunted house," said Benny. "I guess I wouldn't want to live with a ghost."

Everyone laughed, and Benny laughed, too.

"I hate to tell you, Sally," Grandfather said, "but I did say that there *might* be a haunted house in an old town like Elbow Bend."

Mrs. Wade's eyes sparkled. "Now, how did you guess?" she said. "We have a town full of ghosts! And even better, Kate Frances is a very good ghost finder!"

CHAPTER 2

The Ghost Dog of Elbow Bend

"Ghost finder?" Violet's voice squeaked in spite of herself.

"You catch real live ghosts?" Benny asked excitedly.

"But there's no such thing as a ghost. Is there, Grandfather?" Jessie demanded.

"No. Of course not," Grandfather answered.

"I'm not a ghost catcher *or* a ghost finder," Kate Frances said. "I'm a ghost *story* finder."

Henry looked puzzled. "I don't understand," he said.

Kate Frances made a face at her grandmother. Mrs. Wade's eyes crinkled with amusement. "What my grandmother means is that I'm doing research for a special school project on ghost stories. Local ghost stories, to be exact. So I've been interviewing people around Elbow Bend about the ghost stories and tales they grew up hearing."

Lainey said, "After all, just because there is no such thing as a ghost doesn't stop some people from believing the stories, or even thinking they've seen a ghost."

"Are there lots of ghosts in Elbow Bend?" asked Violet, looking around a little nervously.

"They're everywhere," Kate Frances said cheerfully. "It seems like everyone has a story to tell. There's even a famous writer who lives near here who says she has a ghost named Jeffrey living in her house."

"Uh-oh," said Benny.

"But you don't believe in ghosts because

there's no such thing as one, remember, Benny?" Jessie reminded her younger brother.

"Oh, right," said Benny.

"I have an idea," Lainey said. "Now that it's cooling off a little bit, why don't we take a walk?"

The words "take a walk" made Watch raise his head and wag his tail hard.

Lainey went on, "And you can give everyone the ghost-house tour that you gave me when I got here, Kate Frances."

"What a good idea," said Jessie immediately.

Grandfather Alden and Mrs. Wade exchanged glances. "It's still a little hot for me," Grandfather Alden said. "I think I'll stay on the porch a little while longer, and then I'll help Sally start cooking dinner."

"Help is welcome," Mrs. Wade said.

"Okay, then," Henry said. "Let's go!"

Soon the Aldens were walking down the shady streets of the small town. Benny held on to Watch's leash.

Sometimes they would pause and Kate

Frances would tell them stories about the town's houses — and ghosts.

"For example," Kate Frances said, "that house — that's the Pink House." She pointed to a big old house set far back from the sidewalk.

"Is it haunted?" Benny asked.

"Only by the color pink," Lainey told him.

"It's not pink," Jessie objected. "It's just white. With green shutters."

"Ah, but once upon a time, it *was* pink," said Kate Frances, "inside and out. Pink was the owner's favorite color. All the flowers that come up around the house are still pink."

Lainey said, "And they kept one room all pink, too. In honor of the original owner."

Violet rather liked the idea of a house in shades of pink. But since purple was her favorite color, she decided she would prefer a purple house. "Maybe one day I'll live in a purple house," she said aloud.

"With violets all around it," Jessie said.

Violet smiled at the thought.

"Now, there's a house some *do* think is haunted," Kate Frances said as they walked on. This house was smaller, but still big enough to have a wide front porch filled with rocking chairs.

"Is it a good ghost or a bad ghost?" Benny asked.

"A good ghost, I guess," Kate Frances said. "It likes to sit in the rocking chairs on the front porch. People say you can go by on a perfectly still afternoon and one chair will be rocking. Just one."

The Aldens looked at the row of rocking chairs on the front porch. But not one of them moved.

"I guess the ghost isn't out today," Lainey said.

They walked on, up one street and down another. People said hello as they passed and many people knew Kate Frances by name.

"Do you know everybody in Elbow Bend?" Henry asked Kate Frances.

She shook her head. "Not everybody," she said. "But people say hello to everyone

here. They're just friendly, I guess." She smiled and nodded at a woman who was walking by, frowning as she stared at the houses. The woman wore dark glasses, red lipstick, and a big straw hat to protect her from the sun.

"Hello," Kate Frances said.

The woman's dark glasses turned toward Kate Frances. She frowned harder. "Do I know you?" the woman asked.

"No. I was just saying hi," said Kate Frances.

"Oh," said the woman. She turned away and kept walking.

"I guess not *everybody's* friendly," Henry teased.

Kate Frances laughed. "I guess not," she said.

They paused at a corner while a bus rolled by. People were leaning out the windows of the bus, taking photographs, while a man's voice droned through a loudspeaker inside. Kate Frances nodded toward the bus and added with a mischievous smile, "I don't know all the tourists who come through town."

"How *do* you know so many people?" asked Jessie.

"I've been coming to Elbow Bend every summer since I was a little girl to visit my grandmother, Jessie. That's how I first got interested in ghost stories and folktales, I think. I just loved listening to the grown-ups swap tall tales," Kate Frances said.

"Tall tales?" asked Violet.

"Stories that are just so outrageous they can't be true," said Kate Frances. She stopped. "Now, there's a house with a good tall tale about it."

"Tell it," begged Benny.

"Well, during the full moon in the summer, some say, you can hear the sound of a garden party, right over there behind that wall all covered with jasmine. But if you push open the gate and go inside, the sound stops and nothing is there. Close the gate and come back outside and listen . . . and in a few minutes you'll hear soft laughter and the clinking of glasses."

"Ohhhh," Violet breathed.

"Why? Are they ghosts? Where do they come from?" asked Henry.

"Some people say it's an engagement party for the oldest daughter of the family that lived there long ago. Her fiancé went to war after that and never came back and she died of a broken heart, saying that party was the last happy day she ever had," Kate Frances said, folding her hands over her heart dramatically.

"How sad," said softhearted Violet.

Watch gave a sharp bark.

Lainey looked down and then over at Kate Frances. "Watch says don't forget the ghost dog story."

"Ghost dog? Where does the ghost dog live?" asked Benny.

"Oh, the ghost dog doesn't live anywhere. That's a common ghost story out in the country — here, and in other parts of the world," said Kate Frances. "Sometimes it appears trotting alongside your carriage . . . or these days your car or your bike . . . to warn you of danger.

"The story goes," Kate Frances continued, "that once upon a time, a little dog just showed up in town and made himself at home in the shade of the bench next to the courthouse door. No one knew where he came from or whom he belonged to. He was friendly and several people tried to adopt him, but he wasn't interested. So they fed him and petted him and took care of him as much as he would let them.

"Anyway, he watched the people come and go as if he were waiting for someone, but no one knew who or why. They did know that every once in a while the little dog would stand up and bark — just one sharp bark — at someone who was going into a trial. And when he did, that person was always found guilty. People started calling the little dog 'Judge' and the name stuck.

"Then one day Judge jumped up and started barking like crazy, running around the courthouse and jumping up at the windows. People came running out to see what was wrong, and just about then, the whole building collapsed.

"Well, Judge had saved everyone's life. Somehow, he'd known that building would fall. But when everyone remembered what he'd done and tried to find him to reward him, he was gone. He'd just disappeared. No one ever saw him again. . . .

"Except . . ."

Violet pressed her hands to her cheeks. "Except *when*?" she breathed.

"Except when something terrible is going to happen. Then Judge comes back, waiting and watching and barking and howling to try to warn people. And woe to anyone who doesn't listen to the Ghost Dog of Elbow Bend."

CHAPTER 3

Howls in the Night

Applause broke out.

The Aldens turned in surprise. They had been so interested in the story that Kate Frances was telling, they hadn't even noticed that a small crowd of people had also stopped to listen. Several of them were tourists, with cameras around their necks.

"That was just wonderful," a large man with a big camera said. "May I take your photograph?"

"Sure," said Benny.

"Me, too, me, too," several other people

said. Cameras clicked. One man even had a video camera trained on them. Kate Frances laughed.

"Wasn't that wonderful, Elizabeth?" a young woman said to the older woman standing next to her. It was the woman in the dark glasses, red lipstick, and big hat.

The woman turned up a corner of her mouth. It *might* have been a smile. "I'm hot," she complained. Then, almost reluctantly, she said to Kate Frances, "That wasn't bad. You could almost be a writer."

"Thanks," said Kate Frances as the group began to wander away.

The younger woman smiled. "Elizabeth should know!" she said brightly.

"Come on. Let's get out of the sun," the woman named Elizabeth muttered.

The group on the sidewalk broke up and people drifted away. Henry looked at his wristwatch. "Wow," he said, "almost time for supper."

"We'd better head back," said Kate Frances.

By the time they got back to Mrs. Wade's

house, the evening shadows of the trees had grown long and the sun was almost down. Grandfather Alden was setting the wooden table inside the screened porch.

Soon dinner was on the table and Watch was eating a bowl of dog food nearby.

"Fried chicken," said Grandfather. "If it tastes as good as it smelled while you were cooking it, Sally, it will be delicious."

"It is," mumbled Benny, who'd already reached for a drumstick and taken a big bite.

While they ate, they talked about everything they'd seen that day.

"When I grow up I'm going to have a purple house just like the pink one," Violet said.

"But it won't be just like the pink one if it is purple," Henry teased her gently.

"When I grow up, I'm going to move to Elbow Bend and eat dinner just like this every day," Benny said.

"Well, we don't eat like this every day, Benny," said Mrs. Wade. "But I'm glad you like my cooking." She looked pleased.

Watch finished his meal and walked to

the edge of the porch. He pressed his nose against the screen. He tilted his head as if he were listening to something that no one else could hear.

"This town has lots of stories in it. But no mysteries so far," Jessie said. "Not real mysteries, anyway."

"You like mystery stories?" Lainey asked.

"Oh, yes," said Jessie. "We like to solve them."

"Solve them?" Lainey looked a bit surprised.

"Sure. We've solved lots of mysteries," Henry said. "Even one with a singing ghost."

Kate Frances laughed. "Well, with all the ghost stories people tell around here, maybe a mystery will turn up yet."

Just then, Watch gave one short, sharp bark, then threw back his head and let out a long howl.

Everyone at the table froze.

Then Benny dropped his fork, pushed back his chair, and hurried over to the small dog. "What's wrong, boy?" he asked.

In answer, Watch howled louder.

"Watch?" said Jessie. "Are you okay?"

Then, as quickly as he had begun, Watch stopped howling. But the fur on his back stayed up and he kept his nose pressed against the screen for a long moment.

Benny wrapped his arms around Watch's neck. Watch turned his head and licked Benny's cheek.

Looking up at everyone at the table, Benny said, "I know what Watch saw. He saw the ghost dog!"

"Benny! You know there is no such thing as a ghost. Or a ghost dog," Jessie said.

Violet didn't say anything. She stared out at the darkness and the fireflies, half expecting to see a ghost dog float by.

"Watch could have been howling at anything," Henry said. "An owl hooting that we couldn't hear. Or a siren far away."

"Come have dessert, Benny," Grandfather said. "I'm sure the reason Watch howled is as simple as a hooting owl. No ghosts."

Benny looked through the screen at the

night, but he didn't see anything. Whatever had caused Watch to howl had stopped — or gone away.

Later that night Benny and Watch came into Henry's room. Benny, who was wearing his pajamas, rubbed his eyes and yawned. Henry looked up from his book.

Benny said, "Watch and I came to say good night."

"Good night," said Henry. "And remember, I'm just across the hall if you get scared or anything."

"Scared?" Benny said. "I'm never scared. Only, maybe, a little worried sometimes."

Henry smiled at his younger brother. "Well, if you get a little worried, just call me. I'll be right here."

"Okay," said Benny. "And if you're worried about the ghost dog, don't be. Watch will protect us."

"There isn't a ghost dog, Benny. That's just a story," Henry said.

Benny looked as if he might want to argue with Henry. But all he said was, "Good night."

"Good night," said Henry.

When Benny stepped into the hall, he saw Lainey, who motioned for him to follow her. "Come on," she said. "We'll help the ghost dog pay Henry a visit."

"How?" asked Benny.

"With an old Halloween mask I found in the closet in my room. It's a basset hound mask."

"You mean, play a joke on him?" ask Benny.

"Yep," said Lainey.

A few minutes later, wearing the dog mask, Benny walked back down the hall. When he reached the door, Lainey turned off the hall light.

No light showed under Henry's door. Benny wondered if his older brother was already asleep.

If he was, Benny and Lainey were about to awaken him!

"Scratch on the door a little, like a dog, but softly," Lainey told Benny.

Benny scratched on a lower panel of

the door. As he did, Lainey let out a soft moan.

Benny thought he heard a sound from Henry's room.

He scratched again. Lainey let out a low howl that sounded pretty scary to Benny.

"What? Who's there?" Henry's voice sounded as if he had been asleep.

Lainey howled once more.

The light in Henry's room came on. He threw open the door. Lainey howled again, and Benny did, too.

Henry jumped back. Then he realized who it was.

"Benny! Lainey!" he exclaimed.

"No, it's the ghost dog," said Lainey, turning on the hall light. She and Benny began to laugh.

Henry shook his head, grinning. "You almost fooled me. Almost."

Benny threw his arms around his brother. "Good night," he said again. "We promise not to let the ghost dog wake you up anymore!"

Henry rolled his eyes. "I'll count on it. Good night."

"That was a pretty good joke," Benny said.

He went into his room and got into bed. Benny put his flashlight by his bed, just in case, then turned out the light and pulled the sheet up to his chin. He stared at the darkness. Was that a ghostly white shape by the window?

He clicked on the flashlight.

No, it was just a vase of white flowers.

Benny yawned. A moment later he was sound asleep.

Violet blinked and sat up in her bed. What had awakened her?

She glanced at the clock by her bed. It was midnight, exactly.

Just as she realized how late it was, Violet heard a low-sounding howl float through her open window. And then another. And another.

The ghost dog, Violet thought and grabbed the covers to pull them up around her.

Then another howl, much closer, made her gasp.

It was coming from inside the house!

Violet dropped the covers, grabbed for her robe, and ran out of her room. She just missed crashing into Jessie, who was running out of her room, too.

They heard the howl again.

"Benny's room," Jessie cried. "Hurry!"

Henry bolted out of his room and joined them. He threw open the door of Benny's room and switched on the light.

Benny was kneeling at the window seat, holding Watch's collar. He turned toward them. "The ghost dog!" he cried. "It's here!"

Just then, Watch threw back his head and let out another long howl. It made the hair on Violet's neck stand up, almost like the hair on Watch's neck.

More howls from nearby yards and houses joined Watch's.

And then, just as suddenly as it had begun, the howling died away.

Now the night was perfectly still. Not even the crickets sang.

"Watch, are you okay? What's wrong, boy?" Jessie asked. She went to Watch and patted his head.

Watch didn't seem to notice. He just peered out through the window screen into the night.

"What's going on?" It was Kate Frances, with Lainey behind her. They stood in Benny's doorway.

Benny turned to face everyone. "It was the ghost dog," he said. "It was calling Watch and all the other dogs, too."

"What? That's impossible!" Kate Frances said.

"I *thought* I heard dogs howling," Lainey said.

But Jessie said, "Real dogs, Benny. Only real dogs were howling. In the first place, there's no such thing as a ghost."

"It was probably an animal of some kind he heard," Kate Frances said. "Just like he did during dinner this evening. Maybe a raccoon or a fox is living in the strip of woods along the creek that runs across the bottom of the backyard."

"If it was just an animal, Watch would have barked, not howled," Benny said.

"It's nothing to worry about, Benny," Henry assured him. "Why, Grandfather and Mrs. Wade slept right through it. If it hadn't been for Watch, we probably would have, too."

Benny sighed.

"Let's get some sleep," Henry said. "We've got a big day tomorrow."

Kate Frances was frowning. But she said, "Right. Y'all are going to Elbow Bend State Park with Lainey and me tomorrow."

When everyone had left and the room was dark and quiet again, Benny whispered to Watch, "If you see the ghost dog again, Watch, just howl. And we'll catch it!"

CHAPTER 4

Clues in the Park

But Watch didn't howl any-
more that night and when Benny woke up,
sunlight was pouring in through the window. He jumped out of bed and got dressed
as quickly as he could.

As he and Watch hurried down the stairs,
his nose told him that someone had already
made biscuits. He joined everyone else in
the kitchen for a breakfast of buttered biscuits with blackberry jam, along with grits
and ham. Even Watch got a piece of ham.

Grandfather said to Benny, "I hear Watch

did some midnight singing last night."

"He howled," Benny agreed.

"I understand Watch wasn't the only dog in town who howled at midnight," Mrs. Wade said.

"Something made Watch and all the other dogs howl last night," Benny said.

Jessie shook her head. But she only said, "I think I'm going to have another biscuit."

"Me, too," said Violet. "They are delicious."

"When we're finished with breakfast, it'll be time to go to work," Kate Frances said.

"Are we going to work with you?" Violet asked.

Kate Frances smiled. "Maybe we can find a job for you, if you want one."

Elbow Bend State Park was by a big curve in the river. Kate Frances drove past a small ticket booth and waved at the older man inside, who was wearing an ELBOW BEND STAFF cap. She parked the car in a small parking lot behind a building made of rough-cut wood and led the way inside.

"Good morning, Kate Frances. Good

morning, Lainey." A woman came out of a small office right by the front door.

"Good morning, Ms. Hedge," said Kate Frances. "I've brought some volunteers for the day." She introduced the four Aldens.

"We have plenty of work for you. We need someone to stack all the pamphlets in our information booths and to help hand out maps."

"I can do that," Violet said.

"Me, too," said Benny.

Ms. Hedge said, "Kate Frances, I'm counting on you to help me plan the Stories Under the Stars program. It's only two days away, you know."

"Stories Under the Stars?" asked Henry.

Ms. Hedge nodded. "Yes. There is a storyteller who lives near here. She's a well-known storyteller and she'll be here tomorrow night at our outdoor theater. You should come. She's wonderful."

"We will," said Jessie.

"We can sit in the employee section," Kate Frances said. "My grandmother was already planning on coming and I know your grandfather would enjoy it, too."

"Good," said Ms. Hedge. She turned to Lainey and continued, "The ground crew needs a little help today, Lainey, if you don't mind pitching in. Someone knocked over all the litter containers on Bluff Trail and Overlook Trail."

"Good grief," said Lainey. "Who'd do a thing like that?"

"Maybe it was a wild animal," said Violet. "A raccoon. Or a bear."

"No bears around here," Ms. Hedge said, to Violet's secret relief. "And I doubt a raccoon is strong enough to turn over those big containers." Her lips tightened a little. "No, it was someone's stupid idea of a joke."

"Well, let's get to work," said Lainey. "Henry, Jessie, you want to come along?"

"Sure," said Jessie.

"And we can look for clues," Henry added. "Maybe we can solve the Mystery of the Garbage Can Litterbug."

Lainey laughed. "Maybe. Let's get packs from the equipment room and some sandwiches. We'll have a picnic lunch on the trail."

Kate Frances said, "And we'll have a picnic right here."

"See you this afternoon," Violet said. She and Benny went to work in the visitors' center while Henry and Jessie set out on the trails with Lainey.

"Wow," Jessie said as she stuffed newspaper into the litter sack slung over one shoulder. "Some people sure are litterbugs."

It was hot, hard work. Henry and Jessie looked for clues that might help them figure out who would upend all the litter cans — or why. But there were too many footprints on the trail to point to any one suspect and they could find nothing else that helped.

"Whew! That's done. Let's head back," Lainey said at last. "I just hope whoever pulled the trash can tricks doesn't come back."

"Me, too," said Henry.

As they came out of the woods into the main clearing of the park, Henry said, "What's that old cabin over there?"

"Oh. That's one of the cabins of the original European settlers here," Lainey said. "Or what's left of it. In this corner of the park and back through the woods are what's left of several houses of the people who used to live here over two hundred years ago. Dr. Sage sometimes camps out here. She's the archaeologist in charge of digging up the historic sites in the park. Why don't we go meet her?"

As Lainey, Henry, and Jessie approached the old ruined cabin, a woman peered from around the back of the house. "Stay between the ropes," she barked. "Or you'll be trampling on history."

Henry and Jessie were a little startled by this sharp welcome, but Lainey seemed used to it. "Hi, Dr. Sage," she said. "It's just me. I brought some friends to meet you. This is Henry and Jessie. They're staying with Mrs. Wade and doing some volunteer work in the park."

Dr. Sage came out from around the corner of the house. She was a small, strong-looking woman, with dark skin. Her dark brown eyes seemed to miss nothing. She wiped one hand on the leg of her dirt-smudged jeans and said, "Hello."

Jessie and Henry said hello and shook hands.

"So you're volunteering. That's good. Saves the park money. Money saved is money I can use to do my digging and research," Dr. Sage said.

"I'm glad," Jessie replied politely.

Dr. Sage gave a short laugh. "Just don't mess with anything around our dig. It may look untidy, but we can tell when someone's been here who shouldn't have been. People on the tour groups have actually tried to pick up artifacts to take home!"

Jessie and Henry both were about to protest that they knew better than to touch historic ruins uninvited, but Dr. Sage stopped them by raising her voice and shouting, "Brad! You've got company!"

"Coming," a voice called from the edge

of the nearby trees. A few seconds later a tall, lanky young man with long hair pulled back in a short ponytail came ambling out of the woods. Although it didn't seem possible, he was covered with even more smudges of dirt than Dr. Sage.

"Lainey's here to say hello to you," Dr. Sage said.

"And to introduce some volunteers," Lainey said quickly. Henry noticed that Lainey was blushing. When he looked over at Brad, he thought Brad's cheeks were red, too, but it might have been sunburn.

Brad smiled and shook hands with the Aldens. "Hi, I'm Brad Thompson."

"Are you finding anything interesting?" Henry asked Brad after they'd been introduced.

"As a matter of fact, I've found some very interesting pottery fragments," Brad said. "It leads me to believe that I'm on the right track to the town dump."

"Dump?" ask Jessie, thinking of all the garbage and litter they'd just picked up along the trail.

Brad nodded eagerly. "Yes! Isn't it great news?"

Seeing their puzzled looks, Dr. Sage explained, "If we study what people of earlier times threw away, it can tell us quite a lot."

Jessie laughed. "Wait until we tell Benny that the scientists here are studying *garbage*, especially after we cleaned it up all day."

Lainey shook her head and smiled. "I guess we should go and let you get back to work."

"Good idea," Henry agreed.

They all said good-bye to Dr. Sage and Brad. Brad looked up and said, " 'Bye, Lainey, and, uh . . . everyone."

Dr. Sage didn't even notice that they were leaving.

"Are they always like that?" Henry asked.

"Worse," said Lainey with a little sigh. "Brad and Dr. Sage would work all day and all night if they could. They'd be happy if we closed this park to everyone but scientists and historians."

"But you're practically a historian, aren't you?" Jessie asked.

"I'll be a historian when I finish college. Right now I'm just a history student," Lainey said, with one last glance back at Brad.

"Look," said Jessie. "There's Violet outside the visitors' center."

"And Benny, too," Henry said.

Violet had a map in her hand and was pointing to it while she talked to an attractive woman with sleek black hair. The woman had on tiny square-framed sunglasses and bright red lipstick.

Violet then gave the map to the pretty tourist, who stuffed it into a pocket and walked away.

Benny and Violet hurried over to join Henry, Jessie, and Lainey.

"We've given out about a million maps," Benny said.

No one got a chance to answer because just then an angry voice shouted, "Hey! Stay on the paths, like you're supposed to!"

A tall, strongly built man in work pants, work boots, and a long-sleeved shirt that said ELBOW BEND STAFF stomped up to them. He had a rake in one hand, which he waved. "Can't you read?" he demanded. "What does that sign say?" He gestured toward a small green-and-white sign at the base of a tree.

" 'Please stay on the . . . trails,' " Benny read aloud.

"And where are you standing?" the man growled.

Benny looked down at his feet. He looked over at Violet. "I guess we kind of took a shortcut *between* the trails," he said.

"Huh," said the man. "First you walk right through the leaves I've raked up. Then you go and knock over all my garbage cans. Tourists!"

"We work here," Violet said, finding her voice.

"And we didn't knock over anything," added Benny.

The man stepped back, pushed up his cap, and studied them.

Just then Kate Frances came up the trail. She said, "It's true. These are friends of mine and they're doing some volunteer work."

"Well," the man said grudgingly, "I guess you're not tourists. I guess you're not *so* bad. I'm Joshua Wilson, head of the grounds crew. You can call me Joshua. That's good enough for me."

He paused. "But you still have to obey the rules." He stalked off, waving his rake and muttering to himself.

"Wow. He's grumpy," said Jessie.

"He's proud of this park. It upsets him when people don't treat it right. And you can't blame him for being grumpy after someone knocked over all the garbage containers," Kate Frances told them. "Joshua thinks we should limit the number of tourists allowed in here. He says it would be better for the park."

"Did you find any clues?" Benny asked, turning to Henry and Jessie, just remembering the garbage can mystery.

Henry shook his head.

"Not a single one," Jessie said.

Then Benny remembered another mystery. "Hey, Kate Frances," he said as they walked toward the car to drive home for the evening. "Are there any ghosts in Elbow Bend State Park?"

"Nope," said Kate Frances. "Not even a ghost dog."

But as it turned out, Kate Frances was wrong.

CHAPTER 5

Tourists Keep Out?

The next morning, as the Aldens walked toward the Elbow Bend State Park visitors' center, they saw Dr. Sage and Brad. Henry and Jessie had told Violet and Benny about the scientist, and Lainey and Kate Frances had promised to introduce them.

But the two girls didn't get a chance.

Dr. Sage turned toward them as they came up, put her hands on her hips, and said, "You children didn't do any volunteer digging last night, did you?"

"No!" said Henry.

"Why? What's wrong?" Lainey asked.

"Someone's been at the site. Whoever it was made several holes. We just reported it," Brad said.

"May we see?" asked Jessie.

"I guess so," Dr. Sage agreed. "Come on."

When everyone reached the site, Dr. Sage led the way on a worn footpath lined by vivid yellow nylon cord strung between metal stakes. Signs taped to the cord said, OFFICIAL STATE HISTORIC SITE and KEEP OFF.

Brad said, "Over here." He stepped over the cord and raised it up so that the others could duck under. Walking carefully around the edge of a shallow rectangle in the earth, Brad pointed.

Next to the rectangle was a deep hole, with dirt flung up messily all around it.

Benny squatted down next to the hole. "Wow," he said. "It looks just like the holes Watch digs. Only bigger."

"It's no dog or wild animal," Dr. Sage

said. "That's not typical behavior for a dog — to go around digging holes all over the place like this."

"And in just one night," said Brad. "Plus, there are no dog or fox footprints. No animal tracks of any kind."

"Did anything get stolen?" Violet asked as they walked from one place to another, examining all the holes.

"No," said Brad. "In fact, I found several pieces of pottery at one of the sites, scattered around with the dirt that had been scooped out."

"Look at this," Benny said as they reached the last hole, on the edge of the site. "It's a *bone!*"

Everyone peered over Benny's shoulder into the bucket-sized hole in the red dirt. Brad leaned down and picked up the small white object.

Brad sniffed the bone. "It's a chicken bone. From a fried chicken dinner, unless I'm mistaken. But what's it doing way out here?"

"I know," said Benny. He looked around

at the others, his eyes wide. "It's the ghost dog! It was burying a bone — but then morning came and scared it away!"

"Ghost dog?" Dr. Sage's features seemed to grow sharper. "Not at my dig!"

"I know that old ghost dog story," Brad said. He smiled. "I don't think it was a ghost dog, Benny. I think someone is playing a stupid joke."

"If I catch who did it, I'll make them sorry they ever thought of doing something like this," growled Dr. Sage. She looked at Brad. "Let's get to work. We'll leave the holes. No use disturbing the site even more."

"We need to get to work, too," Kate Frances agreed.

They all headed back to the visitors' center.

"That's the second time in two days that something weird has happened in the park," noted Henry. "First the garbage getting dumped all over the trails. Then all those holes."

"It does sound a little like something a dog would do, doesn't it?" Jessie said.

"But it's not," Violet said. "It's definitely a person."

"The park is locked at night, or at least the entrance gate is," Kate Frances said. "Whoever did it would have had to sneak in here at night, and there would be . . ."

"Snakes." Lainey shuddered. "They come out at night. I'm afraid of them. We *do* have rattlesnakes around here."

"Not many," said Kate Frances. "And besides, they're more afraid of you than you are of them. They won't hurt you unless you try to hurt them."

"Huh," said Lainey. "I don't want to try to hurt a snake. I don't even want to go *near* one."

They all thought hard for a moment. Then Jessie said, "Maybe someone is mad at the park. Have you fired anyone lately?"

"No," said Kate Frances. "Everyone has worked here for years, except for the summer students, like Lainey and me."

"Maybe it's one of the tourists," said Henry.

"But why?" asked Lainey.

"You could ask Joshua that," suggested Violet. "He thinks tourists are annoying, remember? He would believe they'd turn over trash cans and dig holes in the middle of the night."

"Yes . . . or maybe Joshua is doing it to make it look like the tourists did it," Henry said.

Lainey looked puzzled. "I don't get it," she said.

"To get the park to limit the number of tourists," Jessie said.

Kate Frances shook her head. "It's an interesting idea, but I don't think Joshua would do that. I just can't see him sneaking around in the middle of the night, for one thing."

"Well," said Jessie, "somebody's doing it."

"Or some *ghost*," Benny said under his breath.

"So it looks like we have a mystery to solve after all," Jessie concluded.

* * *

No dogs howled that night. Benny and Watch and everyone else in Mrs. Wade's house slept without being awakened until the sun came up the next morning.

But when they got to the park, they found Ms. Hedge talking to Dr. Sage.

"Dr. Sage looks really unhappy," said Violet softly in Jessie's ear.

Although Violet hadn't meant for Dr. Sage to hear, she did. She turned, folded her arms, and narrowed her eyes at the Aldens. "Dr. Sage *is* unhappy," she stated.

She turned back to Ms. Hedge. "Well. Do we get a night guard? Some kind of security?"

"I'm afraid we can't afford that right now," Ms. Hedge said. "We — "

Dr. Sage snorted. "Figures," she said. Without waiting for Ms. Hedge to reply, Dr. Sage turned and walked away.

The Aldens promptly followed.

"What's wrong?" Henry asked the archaeologist.

"Holes," she said. She was walking so fast

that the Aldens almost had to run to keep up.

"More holes at the site?" asked Jessie, panting a little.

"No. Different holes," Dr. Sage answered.

"What do you mean?" said Benny.

She didn't reply but just kept walking.

And since she didn't object, the Aldens stayed with her. When they reached the site, Dr. Sage led them straight back to where the first hole had been. Brad was squatting by the dig, sifting dirt through what appeared to be a large strainer.

"The detectives are back," said Dr. Sage.

Brad looked up. "Oh," he said. "Uh, did Lainey come with you?"

"Just us," said Benny.

"Well, take a look," said Dr. Sage.

The Aldens went into the roped-off area. The holes from the day before had been filled in, more or less — but other holes had been dug nearby.

"Take a look around," Dr. Sage said. "But watch where you put your feet. Just because someone is dancing around here at night digging holes doesn't mean you can trample over our hard work."

She stalked away.

"Did you find any clues?" Henry asked Brad.

Brad shook his head. "No. Nothing. Not even a chicken bone this time."

The Aldens examined each new hole carefully. All of the original holes had been filled in with dirt. Now there were brand-new holes!

"Why would someone do all this?" Violet wondered.

"Maybe they're looking for something," said Jessie.

Benny saw something in the dirt. He leaned down and gingerly picked up a small scrap of leather. He held it up. It was twisted and covered with dirt. But even so, he knew what it was.

"Look!" he cried. "A dog collar!"

"A dog collar!" exclaimed Violet. "What's a dog collar doing here?"

Brad looked surprised at Benny's find.

"Wow," he said. "If it's real, it'll be a great little piece of history. This is the sort of thing that you put on display for tourists, you know? Perfect for the kind of exhibits they'd pay to see. . . ."

"Is it a really old collar?" asked Henry.

"Hard to say," Brad mused. "Not very much of it left. It's worn. But it's in very good condition for something that would have to have been in the ground for over a hundred years. If it still had any metalwork on it, I could tell right away. They made dog collars by hand back then."

He stood up. "Thanks," he said to Benny, and wandered away toward the small trailer pulled up nearby, where Dr. Sage was reading on the steps.

"I found a clue," Benny said triumphantly.

"You did," agreed Henry. "And maybe two other suspects."

"What do you mean?" Violet asked.

"I know," said Jessie. "You mean that maybe Dr. Sage and Brad dug those holes."

"That's right. To get some publicity. And

maybe to force whoever's in charge to give them some more money for their research," Henry said.

"And I've thought of one more," Jessie said.

"Who?" asked Benny. "Did I find that clue, too?"

"Sorry, no, Benny," Jessie told him. "It's Lainey. I think we have to add her to our list of suspects."

"Lainey!" exclaimed Violet. "Oh, no."

But Henry was nodding. "Because she likes to play jokes, like that joke about the ghost dog she played on me with Benny."

"That's right," agreed Jessie. "Lainey could be doing all of this as a practical joke, a sort of challenge to us as detectives."

Violet said reluctantly, "I guess she could. She *was* awfully interested in the stories about solving mysteries that we told her at dinner our first night here."

"It could even be Lainey *and* Brad," Henry mused. "After all, they seem to like each other."

"They do seem to like each other," said Jessie. "If Lainey thought it would help Brad's work at the dig, she might help him dig holes to get extra publicity."

"Or even to help Dr. Sage!" added Benny.

Holding up her hand, Violet said, "So we have how many suspects? One: Joshua, the head of the grounds crew. Two: Dr. Sage. Three: Lainey. Four: Brad."

"We have a lot more suspects than clues," said Jessie.

"That's happened before," Henry said. "Don't worry. We'll solve this mystery."

"Meanwhile," Jessie said, "let's get to work. And everybody, be sure and keep your eyes and ears open for more clues. You never know when one will turn up!"

Although the Aldens did just what Jessie had suggested, they found no more clues. It was hot outdoors and lots of tourists were visiting the park. As the day was ending, even more began to show up.

"They're here for the storytelling hour,"

Henry said. "It's a good thing we have special reserved seats."

"Grandfather and Mrs. Wade will be here soon, too," said Benny. "I hope they don't forget our picnic dinner."

"They won't, Benny. Don't worry," Violet reassured him.

Just then they passed Joshua Wilson, who was pushing a wheelbarrow toward the tool and gardening shed.

"Good evening, Joshua," said Jessie.

He looked up. Then he looked over at the people following the signs that said, STORIES UNDER THE STARS. He shook his head. "This place will be a mess tomorrow," he said. "Trampled. Full of garbage. Storytelling. Bah!" He pushed the wheelbarrow away to the shed and put it away, still grumbling.

Benny said, "Look. There's Grandfather."

The Aldens hurried to join Grandfather Alden and Mrs. Wade as they made their way toward the outdoor theater. The trail wound through the woods and stopped at a small clearing. In it stood a small wooden stage beneath a curved roof that looked like a large half clamshell. Facing the stage were rows of wooden benches.

Kate Frances waved at them and they made their way to a section of seats near the front. "Here we go," she said. "Just in time for dinner and storytelling."

"Where's Lainey?" asked Henry.

"She's up at the parking lot, directing people," Mrs. Wade answered. "She'll join us if she can."

Henry nodded.

They ate dinner and watched as more and more people arrived. Some had brought picnic dinners, too. As it grew later and darker, soft lights began to shine around the edges of the theater.

Then all the lights went dark for a moment. When they came back on, a hush had fallen over the audience. Spotlighted on the stage was a small woman dressed in a bonnet and old-fashioned clothes.

People applauded and cheered. And then

everyone grew still so that the only sounds were the wind in the trees and the voice of the storyteller.

It had grown late and the storyteller was just finishing when a mournful howl filled the night.

The storyteller stopped. Everyone froze.

Benny grabbed Violet's arm. "The ghost dog!" he cried.

No sooner had he spoken than someone screamed. A man jumped to his feet and pointed. "A ghost. It's a ghost!" he shouted.

CHAPTER 6

No Footprints

Some people jumped up to look.

But most of the audience just stared as a small white doglike figure seemed to float through the dark shadows beneath the huge old trees at the far side of the clearing.

And then it was gone.

"Everyone stay calm," said the storyteller. She raised her hands. "I'm glad you enjoyed the conclusion of our performance."

"Oh, it was part of the act," a man near the Aldens said in a relieved voice.

"I knew it wasn't a real dog," said a freckle-faced girl with wiry red hair.

An older woman began to applaud and the rest of the crowd did, too.

Benny, who had jumped up on the bench to see better, turned to Kate Frances. "It was part of the show?" he asked in a disappointed voice.

Kate Frances made a face. "If it was," she said, "no one told me about it."

"So it was real?" Violet gasped.

"I don't know *what* it was," she said. "But as soon as we have seen to it that all the guests have gone, I'm going to find out."

Henry turned to Grandfather Alden. "We need to look into this," he said. "We can get a ride back to Mrs. Wade's house with Kate Frances."

"That'll be fine," said Grandfather, his eyes twinkling.

"Good luck looking for clues," Mrs. Wade added.

"Let's go look for footprints," Jessie said. "A ghost doesn't leave footprints."

They turned to walk to the dark trees at

the edge of the clearing. Henry said, "Violet? Are you coming?"

Violet was looking up at the stage, where Kate Frances was talking to the storyteller. Lainey had joined them, as had several other people. They were all talking and several were holding out pens and paper for an autograph. Violet stared at one of the people in the group who seemed familiar somehow. . . .

"Violet?" Henry said again.

"I remember now!" Violet said suddenly. "I remember where I've seen that woman!"

"Which one?" asked Benny.

"The one with the black hair and the red lipstick. I'm sure it's her," Violet said.

Benny, Jessie, and Henry studied the dark-haired woman. She was talking and waving her hands at the storyteller onstage. Then she held out a book and flipped open the pages.

Jessie said, "Oh. I remember her, too. She was one of the tourists who took Kate Frances's photograph the first day we were here."

"Well, it's too bad she didn't take a picture of the ghost dog," Benny said. He paused, then added, "Of course, you can't really take a picture of a ghost."

"True. But you can look for footprints," said Henry. "Let's go."

But although the Aldens searched all along the edge of the clearing, kneeling on the ground to brush away leaves and covering every inch of ground where the ghost dog had been, they didn't find anything that would help them solve the mystery.

They didn't find a single paw print.

"There *was* a dog," Violet said. "We all saw it!"

"A glowing dog that floated along the ground and didn't leave any footprints," said Henry.

"And we heard it howl," Jessie said. She stopped, frowned, and said, "No, we didn't. The howling happened just *as* the dog was floating by here. But it seemed to be coming from somewhere else."

"Another dog was howling?" asked

Benny. "Well, it wasn't Watch. He's at Mrs. Wade's. If he was howling, we couldn't have heard him."

"Hey! Time to go!" they heard Kate Frances call. She pointed in the direction of the car and then she, Lainey, and the storyteller began to walk up the path.

The Aldens followed. They talked about the case as they walked.

Jessie said, "We've heard dogs howling in town. And now we saw a ghost dog here and heard a dog howling," she went on.

"And someone, or something, is digging holes where Dr. Sage and Brad are working," Violet said.

"Someone has also tipped over garbage cans along trails," Jessie said. "So it looks as if someone is working against the Elbow Bend State Park."

"What's that got to do with a ghost dog howling in town at midnight?" Benny asked.

"Maybe nothing. Maybe that isn't part of the mystery, Benny. Maybe it's just a coincidence," Violet said. "And maybe there's no ghost dog in the town of Elbow Bend. After all, we haven't seen one there."

Ahead of them, the others reached the parking lot.

"Look, there's Joshua," said Henry.

They watched as the grounds-crew chief picked up a piece of paper and put it into a nearby trash can, with a glare at the remaining people. He opened the passenger door of a station wagon and they saw another groundskeeper driving. "Thanks for the ride," they heard Joshua say. "I don't know when that car of mine will be fixed."

Joshua slammed the door and the car drove away. Then the storyteller got into her car and drove away, too. Now only Lainey and Kate Frances and a few of the audience members were left.

"There *is* a ghost dog in Elbow Bend," Benny insisted. "Even if we haven't seen it, we've heard it!"

They'd reached the parking lot now, and everyone heard Benny's words. Faces turned in their direction.

"Ghost dog in Elbow Bend?" the woman with the dark hair cried. "Did you say you'd seen it there?"

"No. I've just heard it. I only saw it tonight," Benny said.

Some people stopped walking and turned to listen. The woman turned to Kate Frances and Lainey and said in a loud voice, "See? I knew it wasn't part of the show. I knew the ghost dog was real! And you owe it to the public to tell the truth about what's going on in this town, as well as everything that's happened in this park!"

The woman looked from Kate Frances to Lainey. Kate Frances just shook her head. "There is no such thing as a ghost," she said. "There's a logical explanation for all of this, and we don't need to frighten people with old ghost stories."

"You have to tell people the truth," said the woman, and marched away across the parking lot and down the road.

Kate Frances said, "Great. Why is this happening all of a sudden? I think she's some kind of writer. Probably a reporter.

This'll probably turn up in the news."

Brad, who was standing by Lainey, said, "Too bad Dr. Sage was at that dinner party. She'd have been very interested in all of this."

"Well, don't worry," Lainey said to Kate Frances. "We'll just pretend none of this happened."

"Yes," said Kate Frances. "But somehow, I don't think ignoring it is going to make our troubles go away."

"OOOOooooohhhh! OOOOooooohhh!" Loud howls sounded in the night.

Benny sat up. He grabbed for the lamp on the bedside table and flicked the switch. Light flooded his bedroom as Watch answered the ghostly noise with a howl of his own.

The door opened and Henry came in. "Are you okay, Benny?"

Before Benny could answer, more howls rose up from all around the neighborhood. Dogs all over Elbow Bend were joining in the ghostly chorus.

"Twelve midnight exactly," Jessie said, coming in behind Henry, with Violet on her heels.

Suddenly Watch flattened his ears and barked.

Benny ran to the screen and tried to see out.

"Turn out the light," Henry said. "We can see out better without it."

Violet switched off the light.

Almost at once Watch barked again, a short warning bark. At the same time, Benny cried, "There it is! The ghost dog!"

The Aldens crowded around the window. Sure enough, at the foot of the lawn, a small white figure was floating along the ground, rising and falling.

"Come on! We can catch that dog!" Jessie said. She turned and ran out of the room.

"Get your flashlight, Benny," Henry said. "Let's go."

The Aldens thundered down the stairs of the old house, through the hall, and out the kitchen door into the backyard.

Behind them, they heard Grandfather call, "What's wrong?"

"The ghost dog!" Benny called over his shoulder.

With their flashlights crisscrossing the night, they ran across the long sloping lawn.

The dog was nowhere to be seen.

Watch barked again and raced into the woods.

"Watch! Wait for us!" Benny called. He ran after the small, brave dog, wondering what he would do if he and Watch actually caught the ghost.

They thrashed through the trees, ran through the backyard of another house, and came out on a street. Watch stood under a dim streetlight, staring up the road. He was growling in a soft disapproving way when the Aldens reached him.

"Did you see the ghost?" Benny asked. He dropped to his knees and hugged Watch. "Good dog!"

Violet said, "Why would a ghost run out to a street and then disappear?"

"I have a better question," said Jessie.

"How could Watch smell a ghost to track it this far? Only a *real* dog would have a smell!"

"The howling has stopped," Violet said. "Listen."

It was true. Now the night sounds of crickets and the wind in the trees were all they could hear.

"I guess we'd better get back," Henry said. "But this time, we'll use the street instead of cutting through someone's backyard!"

As they walked back, Jessie said, "It's definite. The ghost dog is part of the mystery at Elbow Bend State Park."

"Trash cans tipped over, holes dug, dogs howling, and a glowing white dog that doesn't leave footprints." Violet reeled off the list of events.

"It doesn't make sense," Henry said. "Why would the dog appear at the park, and here, in town, in our backyard?"

They'd almost reached the house when Jessie stopped. "Let's go take another look in the woods," she said. "I have an idea. But first . . ." Untying her bathrobe, she took the sash and looped it through Watch's collar.

"What're you doing that for?" asked Violet.

"You'll see," said Jessie mysteriously.

Once more, but at a slower pace, Jessie led the way across Mrs. Wade's big backyard on the trail of the ghost dog. "Here, Watch," she said when they'd reached the trees at the foot of the yard. "Find the dog. Find the dog."

Watch immediately began to tug on the sash. He pulled Jessie along through the woods, his nose to the ground. He zigzagged in and out among trees and through bushes.

Suddenly Jessie hauled back on the makeshift leash. "Whoa, Watch," she said. Turning her flashlight slightly to one side of where Watch stood expectantly, she said, "There. See it?"

"It . . . glows," Violet said.

"What is it?" Benny asked.

Henry bent over the dash of white on the

rough trunk of a tree. He touched it and pulled back a finger. "It's wet," he said.

"It's paint," said Jessie.

"Glow-in-the-dark paint!" Violet explained.

"That's why we saw a dog that glowed in the dark," Jessie said. "Someone had put paint on part of its coat."

"It's not a ghost?" Benny asked.

"Not at all. This is proof," Henry answered, holding up his paint-dotted fingertip.

"But how could whoever did this make the dog float?" Violet asked. "And why? And why dig the holes and turn over the trash cans? Why would they want everyone to believe that a ghost dog is haunting Elbow Bend?"

"I don't know," said Henry.

The Aldens began to walk back toward the house.

"It could be Joshua, trying to scare tourists away from Elbow Bend," said Jessie. "He was at the storytelling session, but we didn't see him when the ghost dog appeared. And it would be easy for him to sneak into the park and turn over trash cans and dig holes."

"Yes. He's a very good suspect. But it does seem as if the appearance of a ghost dog would bring more tourists, rather than fewer," mused Henry.

"Maybe." Jessie thought for a moment. "And don't forget Joshua's car is broken. He couldn't drive here in the middle of the night without a car that worked."

"Unless someone was helping him," said Violet.

"Maybe . . . but what about Lainey? She could be playing a practical joke."

"Yes. We didn't see her tonight at all, until after the ghost dog had come and gone," agreed Violet reluctantly. She didn't want it to be Lainey. She liked her.

"Or Dr. Sage, to raise money for the park and her digging project," Henry said. "She wasn't even at the storytelling session. But maybe she didn't come so she could sneak up and make us believe we'd seen — and heard — a ghost dog."

"Don't forget Brad," Benny said. "He was there, too."

"Yes. But again, we didn't see him until after the ghost dog had appeared and then disappeared," Violet said. "He could be helping Dr. Sage — or Lainey."

"We have lots of suspects," Benny said. "How do we pick out the person who did it?"

"That's the mystery, Benny," said Henry. "And I'm not sure how we're going to solve it."

CHAPTER 7

An Exciting Discovery

"I don't have to work at the park this morning, so I'm going to walk to town to do a little shopping," Lainey said the next morning after breakfast. "Who wants to come with me?"

"I do," said Benny.

"Me, too," echoed Jessie and Violet.

"Count me in," Henry said.

"And I've got to get to work," said Kate Frances. "See you later."

Benny put Watch's leash on and the Aldens and Lainey began to walk to town.

As always, everyone they passed said hello. And as usual, it was very hot. They walked slowly, and Watch panted a lot.

When they got to Main Street, Lainey said, "If you want to look around while I shop, why don't we meet again in an hour? We can meet in the bookstore."

"Okay," said Henry.

After Lainey had left, Violet said, "Let's just walk around and look in all the shop windows."

The Aldens soon discovered that the town of Elbow Bend wasn't so different from their hometown of Greenfield. Like Greenfield, it had a hardware store, an antiques store, a bike shop, a shoe-repair shop, a pet-supply store, an ice-cream parlor, and a gift shop.

"Wow," said Benny, "look at all those cameras!"

They watched as the tourists wandered in and out of the souvenir and T-shirt shops and took photographs of one another.

The Aldens decided to walk into the pet store.

"What a cute dog," said the girl in the store.

"He's hot and thirsty," said Benny.

"Could you let us have a bowl of water for him, please?" asked Violet.

"Sure," said the girl. "I'll go get one right now."

She soon returned with a red bowl filled with water and set it down for Watch. He drank noisily. The Aldens looked around the store.

"You have a nice store," Jessie said.

"Thank you," the girl said. She grinned. "It's not my store, it's my brother's. I just work here so I can get free supplies for Squeeze."

"Squeeze? Who is Squeeze?" asked Henry.

The girl grinned even more broadly and pointed.

The Aldens turned. A large snake was coiled around the branch of a small tree growing out of an enormous pot in the window.

Benny took a step back. "Uh-oh," he said.

The girl said, "Don't worry. Squeeze won't hurt you. He's a boa constrictor and not poisonous. Isn't he beautiful?"

Looking at the snake made Violet nervous, so she looked somewhere else. "Oh," she said. "Look, Watch. Sweaters for dogs!"

"Not that dogs need sweaters very often in this part of the country," the girl commented. "Too hot. They don't usually need those little booties, either. Those are for dogs that live in places with snow, where they put salt on the sidewalk. The salt hurts the dogs' feet. I did sell a set of those booties a few days ago. A whole crowd of people came in the store at once, buying all kinds of things. Some tourists will buy anything!"

Glad to be out of the heat, the Aldens began to look around the store. Benny and Watch took a closer look at Squeeze, being careful not to get *too* close. Henry and Violet bent to study the tropical fish in the big aquarium next to the counter.

Jessie let her eyes wander across the pegboard hung with dog supplies: booties and sweaters, raincoats and fancy collars, in every imaginable color; bones and treats; whistles and toys. . . .

She reached out and picked up a small, thin, silver whistle. She held it up. "About this whistle — " she began.

"Look, there's Lainey!" Benny said. He waved, then dashed to the door and opened it. "Hey, Lainey. We're in here!"

Lainey followed Benny inside the store — and began to scream.

"Nooo!" she shrieked, jumping back and dancing from one foot to the other as if her shoes were on fire. "Eeeek. Oooh! A snaaaaaaake!"

Henry raced over and grabbed Lainey's arm. "This way," he said, and led her outside.

"We'll be right back," Jessie promised. The Aldens all went outside to join Henry and Lainey.

Lainey was pale, with splotches of red on her cheeks. "Sorry," she said. "The snake caught me by surprise. If I'd known it was there, I would never have gone in."

"You *are* afraid of snakes, aren't you?" asked Jessie.

"Terrified," Lainey admitted. "I try not to be, but I can't help it. . . ." Her voice trailed off and she shook her head.

"That's very brave of you to work at the park, then," Violet said, trying to make Lainey feel better.

Lainey managed to smile. "Not so brave. I stick close to the trails and places where I know the snakes aren't likely to be. And I wear big hiking boots that come up almost to my knees. When I had to help out during Stories Under the Stars, I worked in the parking lot directing cars. I didn't even come down to the storytelling until Brad came along to walk with me. That's how afraid I was."

The Aldens exchanged glances. Lainey's confession had just eliminated two of their suspects. There was no way Lainey could have had anything to do with the ghostly dog flitting through the woods around the edges of the storytelling crowd.

"Well, you're safe now," said Henry.

"But if you don't mind," Jessie said, "we'd like to go back into the pet-supply store for a minute."

"Why?" asked Benny.

"You'll see," Jessie said.

Lainey said, "Go on. I'll be at the bookstore. See you in a little while."

"Let's go," said Jessie. The Aldens went back into the store and Jessie went straight to the whistle she'd been holding. "I'd like to buy this," she said.

"The silent whistle? Sure," said the girl. She took Jessie's money and counted out the change.

As Jessie slipped the whistle into her pocket, she said casually, "Have you sold any of these lately?"

"Sure," said the girl.

"To the same person who bought the booties?" Jessie asked.

The girl frowned. "I don't know about that. The store was jammed. I just remember selling the booties because it was so unusual, you know? I *think* it was a lady. But what she looked like, I couldn't tell you. I

remember the booties were white, though. Silly color. Shows dirt."

"Hmmm," said Jessie.

"Thanks for all your help," Violet said. "We really appreciate it."

Jessie nodded. "I think you just helped us solve a mystery."

CHAPTER 8

Setting a Trap

Benny's eyes grew wide. "What?" he gasped.

Jessie didn't answer right away. They went outside and Benny hopped excitedly along next to her.

"We know Lainey's not the one who did it, because she really *is* afraid of snakes, and we know Brad was with her the other night when everyone saw the ghost dog at the storytelling," Henry said. "Is that what you mean?"

"Nope," Jessie said. She held up the

whistle in its package. "This is what I mean. This is a very important clue."

Violet leaned forward and read aloud from the package, " 'Silent dog whistle. You can't hear it, but dogs can. From as far away as a quarter mile or more.' "

"Silent whistle?" Benny asked. "How can a whistle not make any sound?"

"It does make a sound. It's just such a high-pitched sound that only dogs can hear it," Henry said. He was beginning to figure out the mystery, too.

They'd begun to walk back along Main Street.

"Can I try it? Can I blow the whistle?" Benny asked.

"May I," Jessie corrected him automatically, just as Grandfather would have. "Okay, Benny, give it a try."

Benny pulled the whistle from the cardboard and held it to his lips. He blew hard.

No sound came out. But Watch jumped up at Benny, his ears straight up.

Benny blew again. Again no sound came out.

Watch gave a short sharp bark. Across the street, a black Labrador retriever veered sharply and began pulling on his leash as if he wanted to run toward Benny.

"That's enough, Benny," said Jessie.

Violet said, "Wow, it works. It really works. And if you blew the whistle enough, I bet every dog that heard it would start howling and trying to find out who was whistling."

"But who would do it?" Violet asked. "And why?"

"I think whoever did it was the same person who bought the booties. The ground was not damp enough to show any footprints — especially with that person's dog wearing the booties. The dog turned into a ghost!" Jessie told them.

"The girl at the store said she was pretty sure a woman had bought the booties," Violet said. "That means it wasn't Joshua."

"That just leaves Dr. Sage," Henry said.

"I like Dr. Sage," Benny said. "I don't think she's bad."

"But she does have a good reason — she

wants more money for her work. A ghost dog means publicity, and publicity might help her get more money for research," Henry said.

"Who else could it be?" Jessie said.

"Wouldn't the girl in the store know Dr. Sage?" Violet asked.

"Not necessarily. Dr. Sage isn't from around here. And if she went into the store when a bunch of tourists were in there, the girl might not notice her," Jessie argued.

But they didn't get to suspect Dr. Sage much longer. They ran into her coming out of the hardware store.

"Hi, Dr. Sage," said Jessie.

"Found the hole-digger yet?" was her answer.

"Not yet," said Henry. Was this all a clever game Dr. Sage was playing so they wouldn't be suspicious?

"Did you have a nice time at your dinner party?" asked Violet.

"Dinner parties," said Dr. Sage scornfully. "I sat there from eight o'clock until midnight with the mayor and a state senator.

I'd better get some more money for my project, it was so boring!" With that, she stomped away.

Jessie raised her eyebrows. "I guess Dr. Sage really was at the dinner party," she said.

"And that means she couldn't have done it," said Benny.

"We're completely out of suspects," said Henry.

They walked slowly on, not speaking again until they reached the bookstore. Lainey was waiting for them by the front door. "Ready to go home for lunch?" she asked.

"Yes!" said Benny, to no one's surprise.

They began to walk back through town, but Violet stopped and stared at the bookstore window. "Look," she said. "There she is!"

"There who is?" Henry asked.

"The lady who took Kate Frances's picture that first day," Violet said. "The same one who was saying she was going to tell everyone about the ghost dog at Stories Under the Stars the other night. That's her picture on the poster in the corner of the window."

"You're right," Jessie said.

" 'Book signing,' " Henry read from the poster. " 'By Elizabeth Prattle, author of *The Lady and the Midnight Ghost*.' She's here signing books tonight at the bookstore."

"Listen to this." Henry read aloud again, " 'The story of a lady haunted by a special kind of ghost in an old house in the historic town of Ankle Bend.' "

"Ankle Bend?" Violet giggled. "Just like Elbow Bend!"

"It probably *is* Elbow Bend," Lainey said. "She probably just changed the name a little, in case anyone thought they recognized themselves in there."

"Wow," said Violet. "A famous author."

"Not so famous. I think this is her first book, and it's not on any best-seller lists yet that I know about," Lainey said as they began to walk home.

"I guess she knows a lot about ghosts," said Benny. "Maybe that's why she was so upset about the ghost dog."

"That's it! That's it! I have it!" Jessie cried. "Benny! You just solved another mystery!"

"I did?" Benny asked.

Henry looked at Jessie. He said, "I think I know what you're thinking. But we need to prove it . . . and I think I know how!"

"How? Who did it?" Benny almost shouted.

"Here's the plan," said Henry. He looked at Lainey. "And we'll need you and Kate Frances to help us."

"Wow. There sure are a lot of people here," Benny said. It was after dinner, and the Aldens had returned to the bookstore to set their plan in action.

The lady standing next to him said, "Oh, it's because of the ghost! Haven't you heard about it?"

"Sort of," Henry said quickly, in case Benny gave anything away.

"Isn't it amazing? A ghost! Just like in the book!" the woman gushed, clutching her copy of *The Lady and the Midnight Ghost* to her chest.

"There's a ghost dog in the book?" asked Violet.

"Well, no. Actually, it's a horse. But it's almost the same," the woman said. She moved away.

Jessie rolled her eyes.

"Look," Henry said. "Lainey and Kate Frances are talking to her now."

The Aldens edged closer, so they could hear but not be seen by Elizabeth Prattle.

"So we were wondering if you'd like to do a reading, as part of our Stories Under the Stars program. Could you do it tomorrow night? I know it's not much notice, but — "

"Oh, I think I could manage that," Ms. Prattle interrupted. She smiled and signed another book, then turned back to Kate Frances.

"Wonderful," said Kate Frances. "About seven-thirty? You can read and maybe answer questions, and after we take a break you can read some more and then sign books. How does that sound?"

"Fine," said Ms. Prattle. "I'll be there."

"Great," said Kate Frances. "We'll start letting everybody know."

Lainey said, as if it had just occurred to her, "Wow. What if the ghost dog shows up again? Wouldn't that be amazing? I bet people will come just to see if — "

"Lainey, there is *no* ghost dog," Kate Frances said sternly. "Come on, let's get to work."

Ms. Prattle watched them go with a little smile on her lips, and the Aldens watched Ms. Prattle.

CHAPTER 9

Whose Ghost Dog?

"The crowd is just as big for Ms. Prattle as it was for the other story-teller," said Kate Frances. "And nobody even knows her around here." She shook her head before hurrying away to help.

"It's because of the ghost stories. The ghost dog," said Henry.

It was true. As the visitors streamed past them to claim seats in the clearing, they heard snatches of conversation. Almost everyone was talking about the ghost dog.

Then Kate Frances walked onto the stage

to introduce Elizabeth Prattle. The audience fell silent, then cheered as the author walked onstage. She stepped up to the podium, took a sip of water, and smiled. "Welcome to all you believers in good writing — and in ghosts!" she said.

With lots of exaggeration and hand gestures, Ms. Prattle began to read.

No one in the audience seemed to mind the exaggeration. They applauded loudly when Ms. Prattle finished reading, and asked her lots of questions. She talked about how her research had led her to believe that many of the ghost stories she'd heard could be true.

Then it was time for a half-hour break.

Henry slipped his flashlight out of his pocket. "Come on," he said to Violet. "Let's go." He and Violet hurried up the trail toward the parking lot.

People wandered toward the concession stand. Kate Frances and Ms. Prattle walked up the stone steps that divided the two rows of benches where the audience sat to listen. Ms. Prattle stopped and spoke to several people and smiled. But she didn't sign any books. "Not until after it's over," she said. "And don't forget, more books will be for sale!"

The Aldens passed Kate Frances. They knew she was offering to walk with Ms. Prattle. "No, no," said Ms. Prattle. "I need a little time to myself. I'll just walk along the trail and think. Don't worry. I'll be back in time to read again!"

She took a flashlight out of her shoulder bag and moved away up the trail.

Jessie and Benny stayed where they were, watching and waiting.

Nothing happened. A few people drifted back to their seats. Benny whispered, "Where's the ghost dog?"

"I don't know, Benny," said Jessie.

Just then, someone screamed.

"It's the ghost!" a woman shouted.

"The ghost dog!" another voice added.

Even though they'd been expecting it, Benny and Jessie both jumped.

Then they saw it: a white figure moving in and out among the trees.

"Come on!" Jessie said.

She and Benny ran toward the dog, skirting the crowd of people who were trying to back away from it. They dashed to the edge of the woods as the dog disappeared into it.

Jessie pulled the silent whistle from her pocket and raised it to her lips. She blew a blast on it. And then another. And then again.

Benny held his breath.

And then the ghost dog reappeared!

It ran toward them. Then it stopped and turned its head as if listening to something only it could hear. It turned.

Jessie blew harder and harder on the whistle. The dog ran forward, then back, then forward.

Benny ran toward the dog. "Here, dog," he called. "Nice ghost dog!" He pulled a dog biscuit from his pocket and held it out.

The dog stopped at the edge of the shadows. It looked utterly confused. As Benny ran up to it, he saw that it wasn't a ghost dog after all — just a white dog covered with something to make it glow, and wearing booties on its feet.

Pulling a collar with a leash attached to it from his other pocket, Benny slipped the collar over the dog's head. "Good dog," he said. "Good girl."

The dog whined a little and looked anxiously over her shoulder. Then she took the biscuit from Benny's hand and allowed herself to be led out into the light.

"It's a dog!" someone said.

"It's not a ghost at all," said someone else.

Jessie bent to pat the dog.

Just then, Ms. Prattle appeared at the top of the stone steps. The dog saw her and strained on the leash, barking and wagging her tail.

Ms. Prattle walked toward the stage as if she didn't see the dog.

And she really didn't see Henry and Violet following her.

She walked up onto the stage and turned to face the audience. She opened her book, although almost no one was sitting down. Faces turned toward her.

"In this chapter — " Ms. Prattle began.

But she didn't get to continue. Benny let the dog drag him up to the stage. Wagging her tail even harder, the dog jumped up and barked happily at Ms. Prattle.

Ms. Prattle looked down.

Jessie stepped forward. "She's your dog, isn't she?" Jessie asked in a loud clear voice.

"I don't know what you're talking about!" Ms. Prattle said.

Henry said, "We followed you to your car just now, Ms. Prattle. We saw you take your dog out. We saw the whole thing."

Slowly Ms. Prattle closed her book. She nodded. Then she knelt down and held out her arms. "Come here, girl. Come here, Dusty. Good girl," she said. And the dog ran into her arms.

Kate Frances said, "Show's over! Everybody go home."

CHAPTER 10

The Ghost Catchers Explain

The porch swing creaked as Benny and Violet rocked back and forth in it. Curled in the corner, Watch yawned.

It was late, long past dinner, on the last night of the Aldens' visit to Elbow Bend. Mrs. Wade had made another special dinner, almost as good as the first one, with peach cobbler and ice cream for dessert.

Now they were all sitting on the porch, talking about the visit — and about solving the mystery.

"I almost forgot to tell you the good

news," Kate Frances said. "More funding is being given to Dr. Sage's research project."

"Isn't that great?" Lainey added. "That means she can pay Brad to keep working for her and maybe even get a second assistant."

"And I think one of the reasons she got the money was because of all the publicity about the fake ghost dog," said Brad. He'd joined them for dinner and was sitting next to Lainey on the wicker sofa.

"I still can't believe that writer, Elizabeth Prattle, would do all that," said Mrs. Wade. She shook her head. "Some people!"

"She got the idea when she overheard Kate Frances telling ghost stories. That was our first day in Elbow Bend and Kate Frances was giving us a tour of the town," Violet said. "She heard the ghost dog story then, saw how the other tourists reacted. She realized it might be useful to her to help sell her book — since her book is based on the same story."

"And she had her dog with her. Dusty. And Dusty was already trained to come to the silent whistle," Henry added.

"That first night, she just used the whistle as an experiment," Benny said. "That's what made all the dogs bark and howl — except her dog, who's used to the whistle."

"And then she went to Elbow Bend State early in the morning and turned over trash cans and dug holes and planted that dog collar to make it look like a dog had been through there," Violet said.

"And then at Stories Under the Stars, she parked her car away from all the others so no one would see her dog inside," Jessie began.

"But wait," Brad said. "How did she make it glow? And leave no footprints?"

"The glow came from glow-in-the-dark Halloween paint," Violet said. "She washed it off Dusty each time. And she put booties on her dog to keep her from leaving footprints."

"Everybody believed Dusty was a ghost," Jessie said.

"She made the howling by playing a tape recording of a dog howling," added Violet.

"And then, after listening to us talk about

the ghost dog in the parking lot, she decided to make the ghost dog appear in town. So she took her dog to the woods along the back of this house and did the same thing," Jessie said.

"Only this time, Watch tracked Dusty, and we found a spot of wet phosphorescent paint on a tree trunk where Dusty had brushed against it," Henry said. "That's when we knew we weren't chasing a ghost but a real dog."

"But how did you know who did it?" Lainey asked.

Violet blushed a little in the dark, and was glad Lainey couldn't see her.

Jessie said, "We had a few suspects. But we were able to narrow the list down and set a trap."

"And we caught her!" Benny concluded triumphantly.

"You sure did, Benny," said Grandfather.

"She got a lot of publicity," said Kate Frances. "But I don't think it was the kind she wanted."

"Her book is still selling well at the bookstore," said Mrs. Wade. "But I think she's sorry she did what she did."

"She sure left town in a hurry," Kate Frances said. "I don't think she'll try anything like that again."

"Well, it's sure been an exciting visit," Mrs. Wade said. "I hope y'all come again soon."

"We will," said Benny. "And we'll catch more ghosts next time!"

"Oh, Benny," Violet said, and everyone laughed.

THE BOXCAR CHILDREN

THE GHOST AT THE DRIVE-IN MOVIE

Created by
GERTRUDE CHANDLER WARNER

Contents

CHAPTER 1

The Diamond in the Sky

Benny Alden was getting sleepy in the car. It was a long ride, and he had just closed his eyes. But then he heard his grandfather say something about...*a diamond!*

"Diamonds!" cried Benny. "Where?" The six-year-old loved mysteries and looking for hidden treasure.

His older sister Jessie looked back from the front seat of the minivan. "Oh, not real diamonds, Benny," she said, laughing.

Their grandfather nodded as he drove.

"I was just talking about the place where we're going," he said. "It's called the Diamond Drive-In Theater." The Aldens were on their way to visit a friend of Grandfather's, Frederick Fletcher, who lived in the countryside beyond Silver City.

"It's so great Mr. Fletcher owns a movie theater!" Violet said. At ten, she was the shyest of the Alden children, but even she couldn't hide her excitement.

Henry, who was the oldest, spoke up. "I've read about drive-in movie theaters, but I've never seen one. I guess they're pretty hard to find these days." He was fourteen and he liked looking up information on the internet.

"There used to be hundreds of them all over the country," said Grandfather. "There were dozens right here in Connecticut, back in the old days. Now there are only a few."

"I bet the front door of a drive-in theater has to be really wide," said Benny. "So that you can get your car inside."

Jessie had to keep from laughing again. "That's not how it works, Benny," she said. Since she was twelve, she was always trying to explain things to her younger brother and sister. "Drive-in theaters are outdoors—right, Grandfather?"

"Indeed they are," said Grandfather.

"And then you sit in your car and watch the movie," Henry added. "So in a way, you're indoors, too—inside your car, at least."

"It sounds so strange," Violet said. "I can't wait to see what it's like."

"You'll see it soon," Grandfather said. They were driving past wide fields, and sometimes, shopping centers. "This used to be all farmland," he told the children, "But it's changing, bit by bit." There were lots of billboards and signs.

The minivan turned left. Jessie noticed a hot dog stand with a neon sign on one side of the road. On the other was a big store that sold new cars. She looked around for the drive-in theater.

"Look!" said Benny. "There's a great big billboard that's turned backward!" He pointed out the window.

Grandfather grinned as he turned the car down a side road. They drove right past the thing that Benny was pointing at. "It's not a billboard," said Grandfather. "But can you guess what it is?"

Violet, who was an artist, had a good eye. "It's a movie screen!" she said. "See how it's all white on the other side?"

The screen stood with its back to the road. In front of it was a large gravel lot that stretched off toward the open field behind the theater.

"It looks like an empty parking lot," said Jessie.

"I think it *is* a parking lot," Henry said. "People must park their cars in rows—just like seats in a theater—and watch the movie."

Grandfather drove slowly around the edge of the big lot, toward a nearby house. He stopped the car, and he and the children got out. Their dog, Watch, woke up from his nap in the back seat. He leapt out happily and ran a circle around the car.

"I'm glad we brought Watch," Violet said. "He'll have lots of space to run around."

Watch trotted over toward the house, which had a big front porch. A man had come outside to talk to Grandfather. He looked almost Grandfather's age, but he was shorter, and more stout.

"This is my good friend from college, Mr. Frederick Fletcher," Grandfather said.

"But everyone calls me Uncle Flick," the man added.

"Are you really everyone's uncle?" Benny asked.

Uncle Flick laughed. "No, not really," he said. "Though I do have a nephew. You'll meet him soon." When he laughed his face turned red, as if he had just been running. "And I got the nickname Uncle Flick because I own the Diamond Drive-In Theater—as you see, I live right next door to it! And I love to show 'flicks,' which is another word for—"

"Movies!" said Benny.

"Will we see one tonight?" Jessie asked.

"You'll see *two*," said Uncle Flick. "We have double features every night starting just after sundown. Tonight we're showing *Island of the Horses* and *The Pirate Spy*."

"*Pirate Spy?*" said Henry. "I can't wait!"

"Neither can I," said Violet. She'd been hoping to see *Island of the Horses* with Jessie at the Greenfield Mall.

"Now we just have to wait until the sun goes down," said Benny, looking up at the afternoon sky. "Hurry up, sun!"

By the time the Aldens had unpacked, the sun was much lower in the sky. The children stood on the porch of the Fletcher house and looked across at the drive-in theater. A few cars were already parked in the lot beneath the screen. The theater was now open for business!

"Flick's already at work," said Grandfather. "Let's find a spot to park the car and watch the movie. We can bring Watch with us."

They got back in the minivan and Grandfather drove slowly up and down the aisles of the car lot. Since it was still early there were plenty of spaces open. But the children wanted to make sure they had a good view of the movie screen. Jessie felt the best spot would be in the front row. But Henry thought that was too close.

Violet giggled. "It's just like when we go to the movies at home!" she said.

They finally picked a spot near the middle of the fourth row. Grandfather parked the car right next to one of the odd-looking posts that stood alongside each parking space.

"What are those things for?" Jessie asked. There were metal boxes hanging on the posts. They looked like old-fashioned radios, and they were connected to the posts by long, thick cords.

"They're speakers from the old days," said Grandfather. "They're so you could hear the movie from inside the car." He rolled down the window. He took the speaker off the post and brought it inside. It had a special hook which he used to hang on the car door.

"Gosh," said Benny. "You mean you had to listen to the whole movie through that little box?"

"James Alden!" a voice called from outside. "You're not going to make your grandchildren listen to the whole movie through that old thing, are you?" Uncle Flick had driven up in a golf cart. He got out and walked over to Grandfather's window. "These days you can listen through your car stereo. You just tune in to a special station."

"Do the old speakers still work?" Henry asked.

"Sure! And some people still love using them. Don't know why, because they sound a bit crackly," Uncle Flick answered. "You'd really be roughing it."

"We've roughed it before!" said Benny. "When we lived in the boxcar."

After their parents died, Benny, Henry, Violet, and Jessie had run away instead of going to live with their grandfather. They had never met him, and they had heard he was mean, so they escaped to the woods. There they'd found an old boxcar, which they'd made their home. They found their dog, Watch, in the woods, too. When Grandfather found them at last they learned he wasn't mean at all, and they soon became a family again. As for the boxcar, Grandfather had it moved to the backyard of their home in Greenfield so they could use it as a clubhouse.

"I've heard you've had a lot of excitement

in your lives already," Uncle Flick said. "I know a golf cart ride isn't terribly exciting, but would you like to take a tour? We have more than an hour before the movie starts."

Grandfather nodded at the children. "Go on. I'll stay here with Watch."

The children were getting seated in the golf cart when a young man approached. He wore a greasy apron tied around his waist and he slouched a little. He had brown hair that nearly covered his eyes. He half-smiled at them.

"Hey," he said. "You must be those kids from Greenfield. Hey. I'm Joey."

Uncle Flick scowled. "He means 'hello,' not 'hey,'" he told the Aldens. "Joey is my nephew. He lives nearby in Oakdale and he works here at the snack bar when he's home from college."

The children waved at Joey. "Hello," Henry said.

"Hey," said Joey. Then he turned around. "Gotta go back to work," he mumbled as he walked off. He seemed either unfriendly or shy. It was hard to tell which.

First Uncle Flick drove the golf cart over

to the snack bar, where he brought out two bags of popcorn for the Aldens. They each told him thank-you as they took handfuls. The popcorn was hot and fresh and with just enough butter.

"You're welcome," he told the children. "We're proud of our popcorn here at the Diamond."

"What's that little building in front of the snack bar?" asked Violet as the golf cart started up again.

"That's the projection booth," said Uncle Flick. "That's where the film projector is."

Just then the door to the booth opened and a young woman stepped out. She looked to be the same age as Joey Fletcher. She had short, boyish dark hair. She looked surprised when she saw Uncle Flick and the Aldens, as if she had been caught doing something she shouldn't. But then she smiled and waved.

"That's Amy Castella. She runs the film projector," said Uncle Flick. "Where are you going, Amy?" he called.

"Oh, me?" said Amy, a bit nervously. "I wasn't going anywhere. Just getting the movie ready! That's all!" She waved again and went back inside the booth.

"She's always very busy before the show," Uncle Flick told the children. "Maybe you'll meet her later. Let's see how the crowd is doing." He steered the golf cart down another aisle.

There were dozens of vehicles now—cars and minivans and wagons, and lots of families. Some people stayed in their cars, but many were sitting in lawn chairs that they'd brought and set up in front of their cars. They had radios so they could hear the movie. Everyone was enjoying the last bit of daylight on this late summer evening, and Uncle Flick waved hello to several families.

"It feels like Greenfield Park before the Fourth of July fireworks," Henry said.

"There are even dogs here!" Benny said as they passed a minivan where a happy-looking beagle leaned its head out the window.

"Yes, we allow them here, as long as they're well-behaved and don't run free," said Uncle Flick.

"That's so great," said Jessie, who loved dogs. "You can't watch a movie with your dog at a regular theater."

"Wow," Violet said suddenly, "Look at that car!"

They saw a large red car decorated with blue and white balloons. The car was shiny and looked brand new. There was a sign on the hood that said BRING YOURSELF TO BRINKER'S AUTO! In front of the car was a man in a suit jacket the same color as the car. He smiled a very big smile when he saw the golf cart and its passengers.

"Kids, this is Dan Brinker," said Uncle Flick. "He sells cars and his business is right across the road from here. Dan, this is Jessie, Henry, Benny, and Violet Alden—they're here visiting from Greenfield with their grandfather."

"Pleased to meet you," said Dan. "I just love coming here and meeting new people and showing off the latest deals at Brinker's Auto. Because what's a better place for car lovers than a drive-in movie theater? I love cars, too. And I love this theater. I love popcorn!"

"So do we!" said Benny. "Want some?" He held out one of the bags of popcorn.

"Why, thank you," Dan said. He reached out and took a big handful. "Thank you very much." He took another handful, and then another.

"Dan comes here three times a week to show off the cars he's selling," Uncle Flick explained. "He has a different car every time. And he likes to hand out all kinds of goodies for free."

"Have a bucket!" Dan said. He handed each of them a bright blue plastic bucket with the words GET SPEEDY DEALS AT BRINKER'S AUTO printed on it. "It's just so you'll remember when you buy a car at Brinker's Auto, you get speedy service!"

"Thanks," said Jessie, who was a bit puzzled. "We can always use…buckets."

"Everyone loves buckets!" said Dan. They all had to laugh at this. Dan laughed, too.

"That Dan Brinker is quite a character," said Uncle Flick as the golf cart went down the aisle. "He's always clowning around. I suppose it helps him sell cars. And he might—oh, excuse me for a minute." The walkie-talkie on his belt was beeping. "I have to answer this." He picked up the walkie-talkie and pushed a button. "What is it, Nora?"

Benny tried to hear the voice on the walkie-talkie, but it was too scratchy.

"Something's wrong," Uncle Flick told the Aldens. "There's a problem at the front gate." He sounded almost angry.

Jessie's eyes grew wide as she looked around at her sister and brothers. "What's going on?" she asked.

"We'll have to head right over," said Uncle Flick, as he turned the golf cart around.

"It sounds like trouble," said Henry.

"It sure is," replied Uncle Flick.

CHAPTER 2

The Sound of Trouble

The ticket booth was at the front gate of the theater. When Uncle Flick and the Aldens arrived, they saw that the woman who worked there was arguing with a couple in a white Jeep. The couple was very upset.

"What's the problem here?" Uncle Flick asked as he got out of the golf cart.

The man in the Jeep pointed to the ticket seller. "She won't let us in to see the movie. All because of some silly business about hot dogs!"

"I'm just doing my job," said the ticket seller. "And you can't bring in food from Duke's Dogs. That's the rule!" She tapped a sign on the window that said FOOD FROM DUKE'S NOT ALLOWED AT THE DIAMOND DRIVE-IN THEATER.

The woman in the Jeep waved a red-and-white striped paper bag, and Benny could smell french fries. She said, "I don't understand. This hot dog stand is right next door! We didn't know until we got here that we couldn't bring in the food we'd bought."

Jessie thought the woman had a point.

"Flick Fletcher!" shouted a furious voice from behind them. They all turned and saw a thin older man in a red-and-white striped shirt marching toward them. "Are you giving my customers trouble?"

"They're my customers, too, Duke," said Uncle Flick. He glared at the man.

"I think that man owns the hot dog stand next door," Henry whispered to Jessie. "His name must be Mr. Duke."

"I know why you made that ridiculous rule, Flick," said Mr. Duke. "You're trying to get back at me...for building my sign too close your precious screen."

Now that it was getting dark, the neon sign for Duke's Dogs was shining brightly. The children had noticed it earlier from their spot in the theater—it could be seen beyond the movie screen.

"It *is* too close!" said Uncle Flick. "And too bright! But a rule is a rule. We sell food here already!"

Mr. Duke had a mean smile. "*Your* food isn't as good," he said. "If it weren't for that rule, Duke's Dogs would put your little snack bar out of business!"

Uncle Flick's face got very red. "Why... you..." he began to say.

Violet had been looking at the Jeep and she noticed something. She leaned over and whispered to Henry.

"Excuse me," Henry called out. He got out of the golf cart. "My sister noticed the license plate on the Jeep is from New York. Are you from out of town?" he asked the couple.

"Why, yes," said the woman. "We're here on vacation."

Jessie stood up, too. "Uncle Flick, these people didn't know about the rule. They've never been here before."

Uncle Flick looked down at his feet. "Yes, you're right," he said. "They couldn't have known."

"We'll be sure not to break the rule next time," the man in the Jeep said.

"You can go on in," Uncle Flick told the couple. "I'm very sorry about the trouble. Enjoy the show."

"And enjoy the hot dogs, too," said Mr. Duke. Uncle Flick shot him an angry look.

The white Jeep drove through the gate into the theater. The children were glad to see the problem was resolved.

"I'm glad they got to keep the hot dogs, too," Benny whispered to Jessie. "They sure smell good."

"Thank you for speaking up, kids," Uncle Flick told the Aldens. "Sometimes it helps to have another point of view."

Mr. Duke spoke up then. "Well, if you want *my* point of view," he said, "one of these days, Flick, that temper of yours will get you in trouble, and you won't be able to talk your way out of it." He turned around and walked back to his hot dog stand.

Uncle Flick shook his head as he drove the golf cart back into the drive-in. "Mr. Duke and I used to be friends. But we haven't gotten along in years," he said sadly.

Jessie couldn't stop thinking of what Mr. Duke had said. What did he mean by *trouble?* It sounded almost like a threat.

***

The children returned to the minivan. Grandfather had brought back dinner from the snack bar. There were slices of pizza, chicken fingers, and bowls of chili.

"Good thing we didn't fill up on popcorn," said Jessie, as she took a pizza slice.

"I never fill up on anything!" said Benny. It was true that the youngest Alden always had a great appetite.

"This chicken is delicious," Violet said. "Mr. Duke was wrong when he said that the food at the Diamond Drive-In isn't as good."

"It's great," said Henry. "But there aren't

hot dogs here. And I could see how someone might want a hot dog at the movies."

Everyone agreed it was too bad that Uncle Flick and Mr. Duke didn't get along with each other.

The sky over the drive-in theater had darkened to deep blue, and a few stars had come out.

"Look at the screen!" said Benny. "Here comes the movie!"

They turned the car radio on so they could hear the movie. Violet and Benny moved up to the front seat with Jessie so they could have a good view out the windshield. Henry and Grandfather sat in the back seat, since they were the tallest. Watch curled up in Jessie's lap.

First they watched trailers for upcoming movies, and then a funny commercial for Brinker's Auto showing Dan Brinker on roller skates. "I love speedy deals!" he shouted.

Finally, it was time for the movie *Island of the Horses* to begin. The Aldens fell quiet as they followed the story, which was about a boy who had been in a shipwreck and was on a raft looking for land. It was so good that they began to forget they were even in the car. Jessie felt like she was in the scene, too, out on the softly rolling sea—

"One-two-three o'clock, four o'clock rock! Five, six, seven o'clock, eight o'clock rock—" The sudden loud music from the radio surprised everyone.

"Yikes! What's that?" Jessie cried. "Did someone change the station?"

"It just changed by itself! And it's really loud!" shouted Benny.

The music blasting out of the radio was clearly not the sound that was supposed to go with the movie. Henry looked around at the other cars. People reached for their radio dials or covered their ears.

"Oh, no!" Violet said. "It's ruining the movie!"

The children got out of the car and started running toward the projection booth. Car horns were honking. "Fix the sound!" someone yelled. When they got to the projection booth they saw the door was wide open.

"No one's there!" Jessie said, gasping. But

then they saw Amy Castella running toward the booth. She hurried up the steps in a panic. Henry and Jessie could see her fumbling with the controls inside the booth. Finally, the cars stopped honking.

"That was strange," said Henry.

Violet ran up behind them. "It's fixed now. You can hear the movie again."

They went back to the car and watched the rest of the movie. The children had a feeling this wouldn't be the last strange thing to happen.

After the movie ended, the children lined up at the snack bar to get ice cream. They were standing near a door marked OFFICE when suddenly it opened and Uncle Flick and Amy came out.

"I just don't know what happened!" Amy was telling Uncle Flick. "The sound just accidentally switched, I guess!"

"Why weren't you in the booth?" Uncle Flick asked her. "You're not supposed to go anywhere, not with all these pranks that have been happening lately. Where were you?"

"I just stepped out for a second!" Amy

cried. "I promise I'll keep a better eye on things!" She hurried off back to her booth. And Uncle Flick walked back into his office, shaking his head.

The children looked at each other. What were all these other pranks about? Why were they happening?

***

"Maybe two movies in a row is a little too much for Benny," Jessie said later on, as they all trudged up the front steps of the Fletcher house. Grandfather carried Benny, who had fallen asleep not too long after the start of the second movie.

"He'll get another chance to see *Pirate Spy*," Henry said. "It's showing tomorrow night, too."

Benny woke up just then. "I like pirates," he said. Then he yawned a very big yawn.

After the children got ready for bed in their guest room, they came back downstairs to say good-night to Grandfather. He was in the kitchen drinking coffee with Uncle Flick.

"I'm so glad you kids could come visit the

Diamond Drive-In," Uncle Flick told the Aldens. "At least while I'm still running it."

"What do you mean?" Violet asked. "Is it going to close down?" The thought made her sad. She knew there weren't many drive-in theaters anymore.

"No, I hope not," Uncle Flick replied. "But I was just telling your grandfather— I think I'm going to sell the place."

"Is it because of all the pranks?" Jessie asked.

"Oh, you've heard about those, have you?" Uncle Flick said. "Yes, we've had a few lately. Someone fiddled with the lens on the projector to make the movie blurry. Someone poured popcorn salt into the soda fountain. That's been a pain! But the main reason for selling the place is just...well, my job isn't as much fun anymore."

"Don't you like showing movies?" asked Violet.

"Yes I do," said Uncle Flick. "But I used to do more than show movies. We'd have fireworks after the show, and contests, and Kids' Night. Things like that were always good for business. And they were fun. But they're a lot of work, too. I'm getting older and don't have as much pep. I'm feeling more and more like this tired and tuckered-out fellow here." He smiled at Benny.

"I'm not tired," Benny said. "Or tuckered out." He yawned again. Everyone laughed.

"But don't worry," Uncle Flick went on. "I won't sell the theater to just anyone. I'm going to make sure that whoever buys this place keeps it open. They'll have to promise me that movie screen will always stay standing."

Jessie thought of something. "What about your nephew Joey? Maybe one day he'll want to run the theater."

Uncle Flick sighed. "I doubt it. All he wants to do is leave this town and—"

Screech!

Suddenly outside there was the sound of tires squealing, and then a *thud*. Watch, who had been napping near the front door, leapt up and started barking.

"What on Earth was that?" Uncle Flick said. He and the Aldens hurried out to the porch.

"It's Dan Brinker's car!" said Henry. "Or at least, the one he's trying to sell."

The shiny red car had driven off the road. Now it was in a small ditch. Some of the balloons that had decorated the car had come loose. The car door was open. Dan Brinker was hurrying about trying to pick up the balloons. He looked pale and shaken.

"Are you all right, Mr. Brinker?" Henry asked.

"What happened, Dan?" Uncle Flick called out.

"It was...it was a ghost!" Dan Brinker said, gasping. "I saw it. Over there." He pointed toward the darkness of the outdoor theater.

"A ghost?" Benny whispered. "Wow."

"I...I was taking the back road. I was driving back to my office," Dan went on. "And then I saw the ghost! It was walking along! And...I suppose I began to panic...and I lost control of the car..." He took several deep breaths and wiped his brow with his handkerchief.

"Do you think it was really a ghost?" Jessie asked Henry quietly.

"No, of course not," said Henry. But he wasn't so sure himself.

"This ghost stuff is nonsense, Dan," Uncle Flick said. "You must have been seeing things! Maybe it was one of those balloons. It's foolish to try to drive with those all over your car."

"I know what I saw, Flick," said Dan. "And what I saw was a ghost!" He straightened up and smoothed his hair. "Now, if you don't mind, I'll be on my way. Thank goodness the car wasn't hurt. I'm just...spooked, that's all."

He got back into the car and closed the door. He started the car and drove off.

"I wonder what that was all about," said Grandfather.

"He sure looked like he'd seen a ghost," said Henry. Everyone agreed.

"Wait—what's that?" Violet asked.

Just then, they all heard footsteps coming out of the darkness behind the road. Benny held his breath. *Was it the ghost?*

But it was only Joey Fletcher. "What was all that racket?" he asked his uncle.

"Nothing," said Uncle Flick. "I thought you'd finished cleaning up the snack bar an hour ago. What took you so long?"

"Oh...I was just being extra careful. I

wanted to make sure nobody was trying to make any more trouble," Joey said. He shrugged and went inside the house.

By now it was past bedtime. Jessie and her brothers and sister went back upstairs. They all sat on the big bed Jessie and Violet were sharing and looked out the window toward the dark drive-in theater. They could see the screen in the moonlight.

"There really is a lot of trouble here," Jessie remarked.

"Yes," said Violet. "So many strange things are happening."

"I think it *is* haunted!" Benny said. "And I want to see the ghost."

"Benny, you know there's no such thing as ghosts," Henry said. "Now let's go to bed."

Jessie added, "Yes, Mr. Brinker was just seeing things that weren't really there."

"Maybe you're right," Benny said. But he also thought to himself: *Maybe not.*

CHAPTER 3

Strange Intermission

"Uncle Flick, is there anything we can do to help out while we're here?" Henry asked. "Besides fixing breakfast, I mean."

They were eating breakfast with Uncle Flick in the kitchen of the Fletcher house. Grandfather had brought back muffins from a bakery in town, and the children had helped wash and cut fresh fruit.

"Yes, we can lend a hand around the theater," Jessie added.

It was true—the Aldens always liked being

helpful. But they also hoped that by helping out around the theater, they could figure out why so many odd things were happening.

"Why, thank you," said Uncle Flick. "There are plenty of things you can do before the theater opens tonight. Pick up litter, check to make sure the car speakers are working, stuff like that."

"I can test popcorn!" Benny said. "I can taste it to make sure there's enough butter!"

Uncle Flick laughed at this. "No need to do that, Benny! But we'll figure out a job for you."

After lunch, the children got right to work. Henry carefully checked the cords on all the speakers. Jessie and Violet picked up litter with special spiked poles. And Benny's job was to bring everyone water and supplies. Uncle Flick found Joey's old dirt bike for Benny to ride. They filled the front basket with water bottles and trash bags.

"You can ride over to the projection booth and see if Amy needs anything," said Uncle Flick.

"I'll head right over!" said Benny. He pedaled off across the lot.

But when he got to the booth, Amy wasn't there. So he got back on the bike to find Jessie and Violet.

Meanwhile, Henry had finished checking the speakers. He went to the snack bar to ask Joey if he needed any help. When he walked inside the lights were on, but the place was empty.

"Hello?" he called. But there was no answer.

Jessie and Violet had picked up all the litter they could find on the lot. They had nearly filled a whole bag of garbage.

"I'm getting thirsty," Violet said. "I think I saw Benny riding his bike over by the snack bar. I'll go find him and get some water for us."

"Good idea," said Jessie. "It's getting hot out!"

Violet walked off across the lot. Jessie looked up at the movie screen, which was shining brightly in the sun. She realized there would be shade on the other side of the screen, so she walked behind it.

It was nice and cool behind the screen. Jessie picked up a few pieces of litter and looked around. She noticed a large bundle near the back of the screen—it was something rolled up, like a tent. She would be sure to ask Uncle Flick what it was. Just then, she heard Henry calling her name, and she went out to the front of the theater.

"Have you seen Joey?" Henry asked. "He was supposed to be at the snack bar, but he's not there."

"No," Jessie said. "What about Benny? Violet's looking for him. He's got the water, and we're thirsty!"

"So am I," said Henry. He turned and looked around the lot. "Look, there he is now!"

They both saw Benny riding his bike near the front gate.

"Benny! Over here!" Jessie called. But Benny wasn't paying attention. He liked the bike very much.

Henry groaned. "We'll have to go over there to get our water," he said. So he and Jessie ran across the lot to Benny.

Over on the other side of the theater, Violet hadn't seen Benny at all. She was still looking for him by the snack bar. She was walking along the edge of the building when she heard a voice around the corner. "Benny?" she said.

But it wasn't Benny. Amy and Joey were there, and they had been talking. They both jumped a little when they saw Violet. Violet jumped, too.

"Gosh! I didn't mean to surprise you," said Violet.

Joey stood up straighter and pushed the hair out of his eyes. "Uh, what do you mean, 'surprise?'"

"Oh...well...I thought I interrupted you while you were talking," Violet replied.

"We weren't talking!" said Amy. "I mean, we weren't talking about anything important."

"Like, why would we be?" said Joey.

Violet thought they were acting oddly. "I'm sorry. Never mind," she said. She was turning to leave when suddenly Amy said, "Wait!" and ran up to Violet.

"What is it?" Violet asked.

Amy's voice was sharp. "Do you see that storage shed over there?" she asked. She pointed to a long low building on the far edge of the theater grounds.

"Y-yes," said Violet.

"You and your sister and brothers need to stay away from there. If any of you go in there you'll…you'll be in trouble. Do you understand?" Amy sounded very serious.

Violet nodded.

"You be sure to tell them," said Amy. She marched off toward the projection booth. Joey went back inside the snack bar. And Violet took a deep breath. She was glad to see Jessie and Henry walking back across the lot.

"What was that all about?" Jessie asked her.

Violet told her sister and Henry what had just happened.

"There's something strange about Amy," Jessie remarked. "She always acts like we've caught her at something."

"Well, she's never where she's supposed to be," Violet said. "Come to think of it, neither is Joey."

"*And neither is Benny!*" said Henry, looking around. "Did he ride off on his bike again?"

Benny had indeed ridden off again. After he'd given Henry and Jessie their water bottles he'd decided to find Violet, too.

He wondered if she was on the other side of the theater, so he rode along the edge of the lot until he saw something he hadn't noticed before. It was an old storage shed. Benny got off his bike and walked up to the open door to peek inside.

What he saw inside made his eyes widen. He couldn't believe what he saw. "I have to tell Henry and Jessie and Violet about this!" he whispered.

He ran back to his bike and rode off across the theater lot. Soon he saw Jessie running up to him.

"There you are!" said Jessie. "You shouldn't ride off like that without telling anyone where you're going," she said firmly. Jessie often acted like a mother to Benny.

"I'm sorry," Benny said.

"It's important," she added. "Because there are places where you're not supposed to go. Like the storage shed. Amy told Violet that if any of us go in there we'll all be in trouble. Okay?"

"O-okay," said Benny. He did not want anyone to be in trouble. So he did not tell

Jessie that he'd been to the shed. He would not tell anyone what he'd seen inside.

***

Evening came, and the drive-in theater opened for the night.

"Are you sure you don't mind seeing *Island of the Horses* and *Pirate Spy* again?" Grandfather asked the children.

"We don't mind," said Jessie. Sometimes the children liked watching the same movie more than once. But they also wanted to find out more about the pranks at the drive-in— and the ghost, too.

"Let's find a spot for the car," Grandfather said. "And then I'll walk back over to the Fletcher house and read my book on the porch. You can call me on my cell phone if you need anything."

Soon the minivan was in a good spot in the third row of the drive-in. It was still twilight, and the Alden children decided to walk around to look for anything unusual. Henry walked with Violet and Benny. They saw Dan Brinker in the second row. Tonight he had a shiny silver car decorated with green and blue balloons.

"Maybe he can tell us more about the ghost," Violet replied.

"Let's talk to him at intermission," Henry said.

"What's in-ter-mish-un?" Benny asked.

"That's the break in the middle of a show," Henry said. "Here at the theater, it's the break between the first movie and the second one."

Meanwhile, Jessie was walking Watch. They were near the projection booth when she heard a voice call, "Jessie?"

It was Amy Castella. She was standing in the doorway of the booth. "Hi. Er...could you do me a favor?" Amy asked. "Could you just keep an eye on the booth while I run and get a soda?"

Jessie didn't know what to say for a moment. Amy hadn't been very friendly.

"Listen," Amy went on. "I'm sorry about today. I guess I wasn't very nice to your sister. It's just that things have been crazy around here lately."

"What happened with the sound last night?" Jessie asked.

Amy looked sheepish. "I wish I knew,"

she said. "But I know it wasn't an accident. There's no way the sound could have just switched like that! I need to be truthful with Uncle Flick and tell him…"

"Tell him what?" asked Jessie.

"That someone must have played a trick last night. Someone was in the booth when I was out."

"Oh, no," said Jessie.

"So will you please stay here for a moment while I get a soda?" Amy begged.

Jessie nodded.

"Thank you so much. I'll be right back!" Amy ran off toward the snack bar.

Jessie sat on the front steps of the booth with Watch. "Amy's being friendlier," she told Watch. "But why does it seem like she's still hiding something?"

After Amy returned to the booth, Jessie and Watch went back to the minivan. As the first movie began, Jessie told Henry, Violet, and Benny what had happened.

"Perhaps Amy is behind the pranks," said Henry. "After all, she lied to Uncle Flick yesterday. She said the sound problem was an accident when it wasn't."

"Or maybe she feels guilty about leaving the booth," Violet said.

"Both she and Joey keep sneaking off for some reason," Jessie pointed out.

"And what about the ghost?" Benny asked.

"Benny, there's no such thing as ghosts," Henry reminded him. "But… maybe someone is trying to make the place look haunted."

"They are!" Benny said. "I mean, maybe whoever is doing the pranks is making the ghost, too."

"That's true," said Jessie. "When the movie is over, let's find Dan Brinker and ask him about the ghost."

Violet started giggling. "Oh my gosh! I almost forgot we were watching a movie! With people all around!"

Henry laughed, too. "But since we're in a car, nobody else can hear us. So nobody is saying 'sshhhhh!'"

"Drive-in movies are the best kind!" said Benny.

An hour later, *Island of the Horses* had ended. Jessie and Violet thought it was even better the second time around. As soon as the lights came up over the theater lot, they set out toward Dan Brinker's car to talk to him about the "ghost" he had seen the night before.

The balloon-covered car was still in the second row. But Dan wasn't there.

"Maybe he went to the snack bar," said Jessie. "Let's go see if he's waiting in line."

As the children walked toward the snack bar they heard a funny sound behind them. *Zzzzt-zzzzt-zzzzt!* It sounded like a bug zapper. *Zzzzt! Zzzzzzzt!* Watch heard it, too, and started barking.

Everyone in the theater was looking and pointing toward something in the sky near the screen. The children turned around and saw what it was. It was the neon sign for Duke's Dogs. Something was very wrong with it. *Zzzz, zzzt,* it went, as it flickered and sputtered.

And then it went dark!

CHAPTER 4

Bad Sign

"What just happened to the Duke's Dogs sign?" Jessie said.

"I don't know," said Henry. "But I'm sure Mr. Duke isn't happy."

"Look, there he is now," said Violet. "He just walked through the front gate."

Mr. Duke wasn't just unhappy—he was angry. The children watched as he marched up the center aisle of the drive-in theater. "Flick!" he yelled. "What's all this about?"

Uncle Flick came out of his office scratching

his head. "What's all what about?" he replied.

"My sign!" barked Mr. Duke. "I know you always hated that sign. So you cut the power to it, didn't you? You broke it!"

"I did not!" Uncle Flick said sharply. "I've been here in the office all along!"

"Then maybe that nephew of yours did it," Duke said. "I've seen him sneaking around the theater after hours!"

"Joey has every right to be on my property," Uncle Flick growled.

"But not on mine! I promise I'll get to the bottom of this!" Mr. Duke shouted. He turned around and marched back toward his hot dog stand.

"Can you believe that?" Jessie said. "Mr. Duke thinks someone here broke the sign!"

"Maybe it was just an accident," said Violet. But even she didn't think it could be an accident. None of the Aldens did. Suddenly they heard a voice behind them.

"What happened?" It was Joey Fletcher.

"Weren't you just at work at the snack bar?" Henry asked him.

"Nah, I was on break," Joey said. He

shuffled past them and walked back toward the snack bar.

The Aldens all looked at each other. They were all thinking the same thing: if Joey wasn't at his job when the sign went dark, then where was he?

The children waited until the second movie was over. The moment the lights came back up, they ran over to Dan Brinker's car. This time he was there. He waved and got out of the car to talk to them.

"Hello, kids!" Dan said. "Did you like *Pirate Spy?*"

"We sure did," said Benny. "My favorite part was when the captain found the buried treasure chest."

"And he found the gold coins!" said Dan. "I loved that part! I love movies! It's been quite a night!"

"Actually," Henry said. "We want to hear about last night. And the ghost."

Dan Brinker's face went pale.

"There have been a lot of pranks here at the theater lately," Jessie said. "Do you think the ghost could have been another trick?"

"You mean...someone wants to make the theater seem haunted?" said Dan Brinker. "Why...yes. Why didn't I think of that?"

"We're just trying to figure out who is causing problems at the theater," said Jessie.

"We solve mysteries," said Benny. "And we're good at them!"

"Well, if you ask me," Dan said in a low voice, "I think that Mr. Duke is up to no good. Maybe *he's* causing all the trouble. He sure doesn't like Uncle Flick."

"Thank you," said Jessie. She was writing things down in her notebook. "That's very helpful."

"Would you like some popcorn, Mr. Brinker?" Benny asked. He held out his bag. He remembered how much the car salesman had liked popcorn the night before.

"I would love some—" Dan said. He started to reach for the bag but stopped himself. "—but I'd better not." He kept his hands in his pockets.

Benny wondered why a man who loved popcorn as much as he did could turn it down. Jessie saw, and wondered, too.

"Maybe his hands are just dirty," she explained to Benny, as they walked back to their car.

"Bye, kids!" Dan Brinker called after them. "Good luck solving the mystery."

***

There was plenty for the children to talk about at bedtime.

"Do you think what Dan Brinker said about Mr. Duke is true?" Violet asked her sister and brothers. "Do you think he's causing the problems?"

"I don't know," said Henry. "The problem that happened tonight was with his sign. Whoever was playing a prank played it on him."

"There are so many things going on right now!" Jessie said. "Uncle Flick and Mr. Duke don't like each other. Amy and Joey are always in the wrong places at the wrong times. And then we have to figure out where this ghost is coming from."

"I think the ghost comes from the haunted house," Benny said.

"What on earth are you talking about, Benny?" Violet said. "What haunted house?"

"I mean, *a* haunted house," Benny replied. "Just a haunted house somewhere. Because that's where ghosts live." He wanted to tell them about something he'd seen in the storage shed. But he knew he couldn't, since he wasn't supposed to look in the shed in the first place.

"Benny, what have we told you about ghosts?" Henry said. "There's no such thing. Right, Jessie?"

But Jessie wasn't listening. She was looking at something out the window of their guest room. Her eyes were getting wider and wider.

"There's...there's something out there," she said. "Something walking around."

"What?" cried Violet. "Where?" She rushed to the window where Jessie was seated. There was another window next to it and Henry and Benny pressed their faces against the glass to peer out.

"It's over by the fence next to the screen," said Jessie. "Do you see it?"

The other three Aldens looked where Jessie had told them. They all saw an eerie figure all in white walking along the fence. The figure seemed to walk and float at the same time.

"It's the ghost!" Benny said, amazed.

"What should we do?" Violet asked.

"Let's tell Uncle Flick!" Jessie said.

A few moments later they were all hurrying down the front steps of the Fletcher house. They ran across the lot toward the front of the theater.

"Wait a minute," Uncle Flick called. He went to the side of the house and opened a metal box that hung on the wall. He flipped some switches. The lights over the theater lot came on.

The children stopped running and looked around under the bright light. Uncle Flick and Grandfather joined them. Watch ran up, too, and barked at all the excitement.

"The person I saw was right over here," said Jessie, pointing to the fence near the screen. "I couldn't tell if it was a man or a woman."

"I saw the person, too," said Henry. "But as soon as the lights came on, he—or she— disappeared!"

"I know it's not a ghost," said Violet. "But it sure looked like one."

Uncle Flick nodded. "There's definitely

something strange happening around here. Your grandfather tells me you children solve mysteries, is that right?"

"Yes, sir," Henry replied. "And we'd like to look around and see if there's any sign of the person who was just here."

"In the morning, that is," said Jessie. "It's much too late at night now." The children looked up at the moon. Even though it was not a cold night, they all felt a little bit of a chill.

The next day, the children searched all around the corner of the theater lot where they had seen the ghostly figure. Henry had hoped there would be footprints, but the ground was too dusty and dry.

"At least there's no litter on the ground either," Violet said. "Jessie and I did a good job yesterday."

This made Jessie remember something else.

"You know, I saw something odd over behind the screen yesterday. Some kind of bundle."

"A ghost costume?" Benny said.

"Actually, I don't know what it was," Jessie said. "I meant to ask Uncle Flick about it."

She walked around the screen and went behind it. The other children followed. "Whatever it was, it's gone now," said Jessie.

"We should still look around here anyway," said Henry.

"It's boring back here," said Benny. He had gone over to one of the two rusty metal ladders that went up the back of the screen. He grabbed one of the rungs and began to play like a monkey.

Jessie frowned. "Benny, that ladder's not a jungle gym. Come help us search the ground for clues instead."

"Aw, okay," Benny muttered. He let go of the ladder. He sat down and found an old white balloon scrap and played with that instead. He stretched and pulled it.

"Hey, look," Violet pointed out. "There are car tire tracks back here. But there's no road or driveway."

"That's interesting," said Henry. "But there wasn't a car back here last night. Look where it was parked. If it were here last night, we would have seen it when Uncle Flick turned the lights on."

"I guess you're right," Violet said with a sigh. "I wonder why someone would park a car back here, though."

"Whatever the reason," Jessie said, "It probably has nothing to do with the ghost."

She shook her head sadly. The others knew how she felt. Sometimes, mysteries about ghosts were the hardest mysteries to solve.

CHAPTER 5

A Popping Good Idea

The children hadn't had any luck finding clues at the theater that morning. They were glad when Uncle Flick and Grandfather offered to take them out to lunch in Oakdale. The Aldens knew they needed a break.

On their way into town the children watched the signs and billboards along the way.

"Wow," said Jessie. "I've counted three billboards for Dan Brinker's Auto Emporium!"

As they drove into town, they could see even

more ads for Dan's business. One was painted on the side of a building. There was even a sidewalk bench painted with the words WHY WAIT? GET SPEEDY DEALS AT BRINKER'S AUTO.

"He's everywhere!" Henry said, laughing.

"He certainly is," said Uncle Flick. "He'd put an ad up on the water tower in the middle of town if he could!"

Grandfather found a parking spot in front of a family restaurant.

"I can't wait to have lunch!" Benny said as they walked up to the door of the restaurant.

"You'll have to wash your hands first," said Henry. "What on Earth did you get on them?"

Benny looked down at his palms, which were covered with gritty red-brown dust. "I don't know!" he said.

Jessie took Benny's hand and looked closer. "It looks like rust. I bet you got it when you were playing on that old metal ladder behind the movie screen."

"Oops," said Benny. "I'll wash up!"

At the restaurant table a few minutes later, Jessie smiled as Benny reached for a basket of rolls with clean hands. It reminded her of something she'd noticed the day before, but she couldn't remember what.

The waiter brought out bowls of macaroni and cheese, bacon-lettuce-and-tomato sandwiches, and salads with big croutons. Everything was so good, they forgot about the strange things that had been happening at the drive-in theater. It wasn't until lunch was nearly over that Uncle Flick even mentioned the theater at all.

"I've got some news to share," he said. He put down his napkin. "This afternoon I'm visiting the bank. I'm going to talk to my banker about selling the Diamond Drive-In."

Benny stopped with his fork in the air. Violet, Jessie, and Henry fell silent, too.

"Is there someone who wants to buy it, Flick?" Grandfather asked.

"As a matter of fact, there is," Uncle Flick answered. "Dan Brinker."

Grandfather raised an eyebrow. "That car salesman? *He* wants to run the movie theater?"

"That's what he told the banker," said Uncle Flick.

"He told us he loves movies!" Benny said.

Uncle Flick nodded. "I know it seems a bit odd that Dan would want to run the theater. But he seems to love the place. And he's a good businessman, too. I trust him."

"Yes, but—" Jessie spoke up. "What about Joey? Couldn't he run the theater? He's almost old enough."

Uncle Flick looked thoughtful. "I would be so happy if Joey took over the business. But I don't think he wants to. He works hard, but he's always disappearing on the job. I think it means he doesn't want to be there. But Dan, on the other hand—he comes to the theater because he likes it. Of course, I haven't made my final decision. That will take time. This is only the first meeting with my banker."

"It's a big decision," Grandfather said.

The children agreed.

***

While Uncle Flick met with the banker, the Aldens went shopping along the main street of the little town. Then they all drove back to the drive-in theater in the afternoon.

As the minivan drove up along the road at the edge of the theater, they saw something was very wrong. There was a police car parked by the snack bar! Grandfather drove straight across the lot to the little building.

Joey and Amy were standing near the police car taking with the policewoman. Uncle Flick rushed over to join them. The Aldens could see that Joey looked very upset.

"There's been another prank! It's the worst yet," he cried.

The Aldens, Uncle Flick, Joey, and Amy walked with the police officer around the kitchen of the snack bar. It was a mess! The refrigerators had been unplugged and left open for hours, and the food inside was spoiled. Someone had dumped oil all over the popcorn bags and ruined them. Worst of all, the cord to the popcorn machine had been cut.

"Joey! Why weren't you keeping an eye on things?" Uncle Flick shouted.

"Now, Mr. Fletcher," the policewoman said. "Your nephew tells me he came in here at the same time he always does, and he found it this way. Whoever did this broke in here hours ago."

"They must have done it when we left to go to lunch," Jessie said.

"Sometimes I come in here early," Joey said. "I wish I'd done that today! Maybe if I had, I could've stopped the person who did this! But I was off working on...something else. I wish I'd been here earlier!"

The children saw that Joey felt just awful. Maybe he really did care about the movie theater, more than Uncle Flick realized.

"It's all right," Uncle Flick told Joey, patting him on the shoulder. "We never thought someone would do something like this."

"But what do we do now?" asked Amy. "The theater opens in less than two hours. The popcorn machine is broken, and we won't have any food to sell!"

Jessie opened a cabinet door under the counter. Inside was a big bin full of popcorn kernels. "Uncle Flick," she asked. "Can this popcorn be popped on the stove?"

"Sure it can," said Uncle Flick. "Popcorn's popcorn!"

Jessie looked around at her brothers and sisters and said, "We've got an idea."

A few minutes later, the Aldens, Uncle Flick, and Joey were in the kitchen at the Fletcher house. They had brought the popcorn and a bottle of oil. They searched the kitchen cabinets and found two very big pots. Henry measured the oil and soon one of the big pots was heating up the kernels. It wasn't long before they heard the first pop! The pops came faster and faster. *Pop! Pop! Pop-pop-pop-pop!* Then Henry started heating up the second pot.

"We're going to need a really big bowl!" said Benny.

"No, something even bigger!" said Jessie. "Big like a bathtub!"

Uncle Flick brought in a very large plastic storage tub. "I just bought it to store holiday decorations," he said. "Though it's not quite as big as a bathtub."

"It's big enough to be *my* bathtub!" Benny said.

When the first batches of popcorn were finished, Henry dumped them into the tub.

"What are we going to put on it?" Violet asked. "Is there enough butter in the fridge?"

"No, and it's too messy anyway," said Jessie.

"I have a better idea." She had gathered things from the pantry—Parmesan cheese, herbs, spices, salt. She poured a little of each into a plastic bag, then shook the bag. She sprinkled the mixture over the popcorn. Everyone tasted it.

"Delicious!" said Uncle Flick. The others agreed.

"Now all we have to do is make a lot more!" said Jessie.

Violet found an old coffee can and made holes in the plastic lid to make a big shaker for the popcorn seasoning. While Joey and Henry worked at the stove popping popcorn, Violet shook seasoning mixture over the popcorn while Jessie scooped it into small paper bags. Then Grandfather and Benny loaded the golf cart with the bags and drove them to the theater. Uncle Flick lined them up on the counter of the snack bar to sell. He put up a sign that Violet made. It said:

No snack bar service tonight.

We are sorry!

But please enjoy fresh cheese popcorn!

Only 75 cents a bag.

By now the drive-in theater had opened for the evening. The customers who came to the snack bar were surprised to see the sign, but they were glad to have popcorn.

"It's delicious," said one woman. "And such a good price."

The children and Joey worked in the kitchen of the Fletcher house for another hour, popping as much popcorn as they could. When there was one last big batch in the tub, they took it over to the snack bar, where it would be ready to be scooped into bags. And Benny had found something even better than bags.

"Wow," he said, holding up two of the plastic buckets that said GET SPEEDY DEALS AT BRINKER'S AUTO on them. "These are perfect for popcorn!"

"You're right, Benny," said Jessie. She spotted Dan Brinker walking by the snack bar. She grabbed one of the buckets and ran after him. "Mr. Brinker! Do you have any more of these buckets that we can use for serving popcorn?"

"Sure," said Dan. "I've got plenty more! I'll

dash across the street and bring them over in a jiffy!" He winked and hurried off.

"Thanks!" Jessie called. She turned around and went back inside the snack bar. She helped her sister and brothers serve popcorn while Joey rang up customers.

Uncle Flick grinned. "You really saved the day, kids," he said.

"We're glad we could help," said Violet.

"Maybe I can help, too," said a voice from the doorway of the snack bar. It was Mr. Duke. He was carrying a cooler and a bag of ice. "I...I heard what happened. And I brought over some soda from my stand."

Uncle Flick scratched his head. "Why, thank you, Duke. But you know, I'm letting folks bring in food from your place tonight. You didn't have to do this."

"I know," Mr. Duke said. "But I'm sorry about last night, too. I lost my temper. And I know that you didn't break my sign." He lugged the cooler and ice to the snack bar counter.

"Yes," said Uncle Flick. "Whoever's playing tricks around here is playing them on both of us."

As the Aldens scooped bags of popcorn, Mr. Duke and Uncle Flick opened sodas and filled cups with ice. The children listened as the two men talked for the first time in a long time.

"Is it true you might sell the theater, Flick?" Mr. Duke asked, as he got ready to leave.

"Yes it is," Uncle Flick replied. "But I'm going to make sure it doesn't close down."

"That's good to hear," said Mr. Duke. "Because I can't imagine life without the Diamond Drive-In. I don't know what would happen to my hot dog stand if the theater wasn't around." He chuckled. "Though it's not going to be as much fun without you around to argue with."

Uncle Flick laughed, too.

Henry whispered to Jessie, "We're not any closer to solving the mystery," he said. "But at least we've helped fix a friendship."

CHAPTER 6

What Everyone Wants

A half hour later, the popcorn the Aldens made was still selling well. So well, in fact, that they were running out of containers to serve it in. Violet looked at the crowd in the snack bar and began to worry.

"Shouldn't Dan Brinker be here by now, Jessie? You said he was bringing more buckets for us to use," she said.

Jessie looked at her watch. "I guess something came up at his store," she said. "I'll go to Duke's Dogs and see if I can get some spare bags." She was sure that Mr. Duke would be helpful, now that he and Uncle Flick were friendly again. She hurried out the door and ran across the lot.

Not too long after she left, Uncle Flick turned to the other children. "Why don't you get a soda, kids? Joey and I can take it from here. You've done plenty."

Henry, Violet, and Benny were glad to have a break. They walked out to the theater lot with their sodas. There was a small playground at the front of the theater near the screen, and they sat on the swings and watched the sun set.

"Why does everyone have to wait until dark to watch the movie?" Benny asked. "At home we don't need to turn out the lights to watch TV."

"Watching a movie in a theater isn't the same as TV," Henry explained. "The projector throws flickering light on a screen. The darkness makes this easier to see. But if the sun was out—or if the lights were on—it would be much harder to see the movie."

Violet was thinking about this. "That's sort

of like the ghost!" she said. "Remember how we couldn't see it when Uncle Flick turned on the lights out here in the theater?"

"You're right," said Henry. "Maybe this ghost is just...made of light somehow. We'll have to get closer next time we see it."

"And we won't turn on the lights and scare it away!" said Benny.

Meanwhile, Jessie was at Duke's Dogs, hoping Mr. Duke had some spare bags that they could use for popcorn.

"Of course I've got extra bags," Mr. Duke told her. "Let me get them."

Jessie looked around the hot dog stand while she waited. There were plenty of customers eating at picnic tables. One of them looked familiar. It was Dan Brinker. He had three empty hot dog wrappers and a half-eaten tray of fries in front of him. He was reading a magazine. It looked like he'd been sitting and eating for a long time. Why hadn't he brought over the buckets like he'd said he would?

Maybe he forgot, Jessie thought. *Or maybe he made a mistake and didn't have any after all.*

She wondered if she should ask him. But then Dan had started to talk to a young woman in a Duke's Dogs uniform. He laughed and joked with her as she picked up the wrappers from his table. Just then, Mr. Duke brought out a bundle of paper bags for Jessie.

"Thank you, Mr. Duke," she told him.

As she hurried out she overheard just a little bit of Dan Brinker's conversation with the young woman. "If you ask me," he was saying, "I think that Flick is up to no good."

***

After all the popcorn-making, the Alden children were tired. They went back to the Fletcher house. Grandfather brought them sandwiches on the porch, and they sat on the steps with Watch. They all ate and looked out over the theater filled with cars. Tonight, the first movie was *Pirate Spy*. They could see it on the giant screen in the distance.

"It almost doesn't matter that we can't hear the movie from here," Henry said. "We've seen it twice already!"

"And we know the story," said Violet. "I wish we could say the same for this mystery.

So many things are happening! I'm sure it all fits together somehow—but how?"

Jessie nodded. "I know what you mean. It's like when we watched this movie for the first time," she said, pointing toward the screen. "We didn't know why the pirate captain was acting so strangely. We didn't know it was because he wanted to steal the diamond ring for himself."

"But then, the second time we saw the movie, we knew he never took off his boots for a *reason*," said Henry. "He'd hidden the ring there! It made sense once we knew what he wanted."

Jessie had an idea just then. She took out her notebook and opened it to a new page.

"What does everyone want?" she asked. "Everyone involved in this mystery, that is. Maybe if we thought about that, it would help."

"I think you're right, Jessie," said Henry.

So Jessie wrote WHAT EVERYONE WANTS at the top of the page.

"Let's start with Amy," she said.

"She seems worried about the theater. She wants...to keep her job, I guess," said

Violet. "And she wants us to stay away from that shed."

Benny wanted very much to say something about the shed. Should he? he wondered. But he took another big bite of sandwich instead.

"What about Joey?" asked Violet.

"I think Joey wants to help Uncle Flick," Henry said. "Even if Uncle Flick doesn't think so."

Jessie wrote that down, too. She bit her pencil as she thought. "What if Joey wants to make trouble for Mr. Duke? Maybe he thinks that would help Uncle Flick," she said.

"I guess that's possible," said Henry. "But we don't know for sure. So write it down with a question mark."

So Jessie did. Next she wrote DAN BRINKER on the page. "What does *he* want?"

"To sell cars!" Benny said. "And put ads up all over town!"

Violet giggled. "He wants 'speedy deals!'" she said.

"And he wants to run the theater, too," Henry added.

Jessie wrote it all down. Soon she had a list:

WHAT EVERYONE WANTS

AMY— Wants to keep her job.

Wants us to stay away from shed.

JOEY— Wants to help Uncle Flick.

Wants to make trouble for Mr. Duke???

DAN BRINKER—Wants to sell cars.

Wants "speedy deals."

Wants to put ads all over town.

Wants to run the theater.

MR. DUKE: Wants to stay in business.

Wants theater to stay open, too.

UNCLE FLICK: Wants to sell the theater.

"Dan Brinker wants to do lots of things," Violet said, looking at the list.

"Dan Brinker *says* lots of things, too," Jessie said. She told her sister and brothers what she'd overheard at Duke's Dogs. "He said he thought Uncle Flick was up to no good."

"Wait a minute," said Henry. "He told us the same thing about Mr. Duke last night, remember? So whose side is he on?"

"I would think he'd have to be on *both* their sides," said Violet. "He wants to buy the theater from Uncle Flick. And he needs to get along with Mr. Duke next door."

"Well, maybe he didn't really mean what he said," Jessie said. "Maybe he says things that he thinks other people *want* to hear. He seems very good at that."

"But he's not good at watching movies!" Benny said suddenly. The other children turned and looked at him. What on Earth did he mean?

Benny pointed to the movie screen. It showed the scene in *Pirate Spy* when the captain found the buried treasure chest. The captain grinned as he dug it out of the sand.

"Remember when I told Dan Brinker that this was my favorite scene?" Benny asked. "Then he said he liked it too. He said he liked when the captain opened up the chest and found the gold! But that's not what really happened in the movie. Look!"

The children watched the movie as the captain opened the treasure chest. His smile vanished. The chest was empty!

"That's right!" Henry exclaimed. "We all thought there would be gold in the chest—but there wasn't! Dan must have forgotten about that part of the movie."

"But it's a really important part of the movie," said Jessie. "It changes the whole story. And Dan Brinker has seen the movie more than once—just like us!"

"Maybe he didn't really watch it closely," said Violet. "Maybe he was busy doing something else."

Jessie wrote that down in her notebook, too. Then she looked at the list again. "Now we know what everyone wants, but we still don't know what's going on! Or what this has to do with the ghost!"

"Maybe it'll all make sense later," said Henry. "And as for the ghost, I think we should go look for it tonight."

CHAPTER 7

To Catch a Ghost

It was late when the second movie ended and the last of the cars had left the drive-in theater. Uncle Flick had returned to the house, and all seemed quiet outside.

Watch stood at the door to the porch. He wanted to go for one last walk before bedtime.

"We'll take him," Jessie told Grandfather. The children put on their shoes and found their flashlights. Jessie picked up Watch's leash. Then they walked across the lawn of the Fletcher house toward the theater.

Everything was dark—except for the neon sign that read DUKE'S DOGS. It shone brightly in the distance.

"Look, Mr. Duke's sign is fixed!" said Violet. "We were so busy tonight we didn't even notice."

The children and Watch walked toward the sign to get a closer look. When they had gotten as close as they could, they were behind the movie screen. They were close enough to the road to hear cars going by. Though it was night, the Aldens didn't need their flashlights, because the pink and orange glow of the big neon sign was so bright. It lit up the back of the screen.

"Wow," said Jessie. "The other day I thought that someone was hiding something back here. But it's too bright to hide anything! You can see almost everything from the road."

"But wait," Violet said. "What if that's why the sign was broken last night?"

Henry thought about this. "That's possible. All along we've thought someone broke the sign to make Mr. Duke angry. But maybe somebody wanted it to be dark back here."

"But why?" Jessie said. "There's nothing here." She looked on the ground by the screen. Nothing.

Violet wasn't looking at the ground. She was looking up and she saw something along the top of the screen. *Had that always been there?* she wondered. It was high up and hard to see. She wanted to look closer. But then Benny made her forget what she was doing.

"Ghost!" he said, in a very loud whisper. *"Ghost!"* Watch started barking, too.

The children turned and saw the ghostly figure. It walked along a fence in the theater lot. The children hurried out to see it better. But while Jessie, Violet, and Benny raced toward the ghost, Henry did not. He turned and ran toward the projection booth.

"Hey!" he called. The others stopped and watched him as he ran up the steps of the booth and threw open the door.

"Henry, what are you doing?" Violet yelled.

Amy and Joey were in the booth. The film projector was on. Amy gasped and then reached over to turn it off. As soon as she did, the ghost disappeared.

"I knew it!" said Henry. The other children had run up to join him. "I knew the ghost had to be a movie of some kind."

Jessie glared at Amy and Joey. "Why were you doing that? Why were you trying to make the theater seem haunted?" she said.

"I know why!" Benny said. But he wasn't able to finish. Just then, Uncle Flick drove up in his golf cart with Grandfather.

"What's all this about?" he said to Amy and Joey. "I heard voices out here, and I saw this 'ghost' of yours. What are you two up to?" he was very angry.

"We can explain," said Joey.

"You'll do no such thing!" growled Uncle Flick. "I've had it! You're done here! You're—"

"Wait!" Benny yelled. He turned to Joey and Amy. "Tell him!" he said. "Tell Uncle Flick about the haunted house!"

"What?" said Jessie.

"How did you know?" said Amy.

Haunted house?!" said Uncle Flick. "What are you talking about?"

"I'll show you!" said Benny. "Follow me!"

***

Benny led them all to the storage shed, where Amy had told the children not to go. Benny pulled open the door.

"Turn on the light!" he said to Joey.

Joey did. And the children couldn't believe what was inside.

"Yikes! A huge spider!" Violet said. Then she laughed.

"Oh my gosh, look at that bat!" Jessie exclaimed. And she laughed, too.

"Wow, that mummy is amazing!" said Benny.

The shed was filled with all kinds of haunted house things—fake skeletons, cobwebs, and plastic bats hanging from the ceiling. There were spooky gravestones made from painted wood, and even a casket with a lid that lifted to show a mummy inside.

"This stuff is even better than the haunted house they have every year at the Greenfield Town Hall!" Henry said.

Amy grinned. "We've been working on it for two months," she said.

"It's very impressive," said Grandfather. "But what's it all for? And why were you keeping it secret?"

Joey pushed the hair out of his eyes. He turned to Uncle Flick. "Well, see, Amy and I had this idea to do a special event here at the theater this fall. We would call it 'Haunted House Days' and open the theater during the day."

"And at night we would show monster movies. And have hayrides," said Amy.

"And we'd decorate the whole theater with all this spooky stuff and special effects. But..." said Joey.

"Go on," said Uncle Flick.

"We were afraid that you wouldn't want to do it. We were worried you'd think it was too much work. So we decided to do it all by ourselves and surprise you," Joey said.

"During the day, we worked on making things here in the shed," said Amy. "And at night, we tested out the 'ghost' special effect. I'm a film student at college, so I made a short movie of Joey walking around draped in a sheet. Then we projected it against the fence so that it looked like a ghost."

"It really *did* look like one," Jessie said. The other children agreed.

"But we never meant to scare anyone for real," said Amy. "We're so sorry about that."

Joey looked down at his feet. "And we're sorry we haven't been keeping a better eye on things. If I hadn't been here painting stuff maybe the snack bar wouldn't have been vandalized."

"It's not your fault, Joey," said Uncle Flick. He didn't look angry now. He had a wistful smile. "I just wished you'd told me about your ideas. All along I thought you weren't interested in helping run the Diamond Drive-In. I wish I'd known before I decided to sell it." He sighed. "But this 'Haunted House Days' is a fine idea. It'll be a good thing to do at the end of the season. It'll be a great way to say good-bye to the theater."

Joey and Amy looked at each other, and then at the Aldens. They were wistful, too.

"Yes," said Joey. "It will."

CHAPTER 8

Speedy Deals

It was Monday morning, the last full day of the Aldens' visit. Tomorrow morning they would return to Greenfield. Since the Diamond Drive-In was closed on Mondays, they had the day all to themselves.

"I'm going over to Dan Brinker's auto store this morning," said Grandfather at breakfast. "Would you kids like to come along?"

"Are we going to get a new car?" Benny asked.

"No, not this year," Grandfather said. "But

sometimes it's fun to look at the latest models."

"Good idea," said Jessie. The other children nodded.

So they all went across the road to the car dealership. It was in a big glass building surrounded by rows and rows of shiny cars. It seemed more like a circus than a store. There were balloons everywhere, and bright painted signs that said GREAT DEALS! All the salespeople wore red jackets. There was a huge showroom with cars on display. The Aldens liked getting into each one and smelling the new car smell.

Dan Brinker seemed very glad to see them. "So! Are you looking for a family car? I love families!"

"Oh, we can't buy anything right now," Grandfather said. "We're happy with the car we have now. But I just like to see the new models! Please don't mind us—we're just looking."

"Ah, yes, it's good to plan ahead," said Dan. He was very friendly. But he also followed Grandfather all around the showroom.

"This is the hottest style around," he told

Grandfather, pointing to a bright yellow car. "We've got two left. I'll give you a special low price so you can drive it home today!"

Grandfather shook his head. "As I said before, I'm not interested in buying today. Or even this year."

"I know you don't *need* a car now," Dan replied. "But you might need one next year. And if you get it now, you'll be planning ahead!"

"No, thank you," Grandfather said firmly.

Dan turned to the children. "I bet you kids want a new car, don't you?"

"No, that's okay," said Jessie. "But speaking of buying, is it true you're going to buy the Diamond Drive-In Theater?"

"Yes, indeed!" said the car salesman. "I love the Diamond!"

"So you're going to keep the place open as a drive-in theater?" Henry asked.

Dan smiled. "I promised Flick Fletcher that the screen would always stay standing," he said.

The children wanted to ask Dan Brinker more questions. But one of his employees walked up and handed him a cordless phone.

"It's the bank," the man said.

"Sorry, kids," Dan told the Aldens. "I've been waiting for this important call." He leaned against one of the cars and started to talk on the phone.

Grandfather wanted to look at some of the new cars in the lot outside, so the Aldens walked toward the door. As they were leaving, Dan started to shout into the phone.

"What do you mean he wants a little more time? I want to buy it now! No...I've planned ahead for this deal! I want it to be speedy!" He sounded upset. The children didn't hear the rest, though. It would have been rude to listen in. But they couldn't help but wonder if he was talking about the Diamond Drive-In Theater.

"Why is he in such a hurry?" Jessie wondered.

"Maybe he just likes to do everything fast," Violet said. "He sure talks fast."

As the Aldens got back into the minivan, a saleswoman in a red jacket waved good-bye.

"Come back to Brinker's Auto Store soon!" she said. "We're the biggest place in town to buy a car. And we're getting even bigger!"

***

They had just finished lunch at Uncle Flick's house when there was an urgent knock on the door. It was Mr. Duke.

"Flick! I heard a rumor that you're selling the theater to Dan Brinker!" he said as he marched into the kitchen where the Aldens were clearing the table.

"Yes, we're discussing it," said Uncle Flick.

Mr. Duke shook his head. "Are you crazy? Are you sure he's not planning to shut it down and turn it into another sales lot? He's just across the street! How do you know he's going to keep it open?"

"Well, because he said so," Uncle Flick replied. "He knows I wouldn't sell it to him unless he swore that the movie screen would stay standing. And that's just what he promised."

Mr. Duke scratched his head. "I don't know," he said. "I just don't quite trust him. Maybe you should think about this."

"I'm not going to rush into this, if that's what you're worried about." He patted Mr.

Duke on the back.

"That's good to know," said Mr. Duke. "Because if you change your mind about selling the theater to Dan Brinker, you can always sell it to me."

Uncle Flick's eyes narrowed. "What do you mean, Duke?" His voice sounded cold.

Mr. Duke tried to explain. "Nothing! I...I mean...I wish you weren't selling the theater in the first place. But if you need someone trustworthy to buy it, someone who will keep it going...*I* could buy it. That's all I'm saying." He stepped back. The children could see he hadn't meant to make Uncle Flick angry.

"Oh, is *that* what you want?" said Uncle Flick. "To take this place over? Is that why you've been playing all those pranks? You've been trying to drive me to sell the place, haven't you?!"

Now it was Mr. Duke's turn to get angry. "Now, Flick, you *know* that wasn't me. I would never do that! We've been working next door to each other for thirty years! We haven't always gotten along, but how dare you think

I'd play tricks!" Mr. Duke turned around and walked out of the kitchen. A moment later everyone heard the door slam.

Uncle Flick's face was red. He took a deep breath. "I'm sorry. I guess we lost our tempers."

Grandfather put his hand on his old friend's shoulder. "Flick, do you want to go for a walk?"

"We can finish cleaning up here," Jessie offered.

Finally Uncle Flick managed a smile. "Thanks, folks. Yes, perhaps I need to take a walk. And think." He left the room with Grandfather. After a moment the children saw them walking down the road toward the drive-in.

"We may have solved the mystery of the ghost at the drive-in," Henry said, "but we still haven't figured out who's behind the pranks."

The oldest Alden was right. They still hadn't found out who had switched the movie sound the other night, or broken the Duke's Dogs sign, or vandalized the snack bar.

"Someone's trying to ruin everything,"

Benny said.

"We'll just have to stop that someone," Jessie replied.

CHAPTER 9

The Truth Unfolds

Henry, Jessie, Violet, and Benny sat around the kitchen table. Jessie had her notebook open to a new page. On it was a list of names she'd written:

AMY

JOEY

DAN BRINKER

MR. DUKE

One of these people, the children were sure, had been causing the trouble at the Diamond Drive-In Theater.

Violet pointed to Amy's and Joey's names. "I don't think they did it. I think they want to save the theater."

Everyone else agreed. So Jessie crossed Amy and Joey off the list.

"What about that argument we heard today?" Henry asked. "Do you think that Mr. Duke is really trying to force Uncle Flick to sell him the theater?"

"No," Jessie said. She tapped her pen, because she was thinking hard.

"I don't think so, either," said Violet. Benny nodded, too.

Jessie kept tapping her pen. "But...but what if Dan Brinker is? What if *he's* the one who's doing all the pranks?"

Henry shook his head. "That doesn't make sense, Jessie. Uncle Flick already likes Dan and *wants* to sell the theater to him. Dan doesn't have to make him do anything."

"That's true," said Jessie. "But there's something about Dan Brinker that I don't trust. For one thing, he said he would help us with the popcorn last night. He said he had extra buckets. But then he never brought them!"

"Perhaps he just didn't have any extras after all," Violet said. "Who's to say he didn't want to help us?" She always tried to think the best about people.

Henry looked thoughtful. "Well, if you think about it, whoever wrecked the snack bar certainly wouldn't want to help us."

"Do you think that 'whoever' was Dan?" Jessie asked.

"Who knows? There's no way we can prove it," Henry said. "All we can do is think of reasons why he'd play pranks."

"Maybe he just wanted Uncle Flick to sell him the theater faster!" Benny said. "He likes speedy deals! Remember we wrote it down?"

"Very good, Benny," Jessie said. Then she flipped back in her notebook to the WHAT EVERYONE WANTS page. "Here's another note I wrote down other night: 'Dan Brinker says things that other people like to hear.' "

"Gosh," said Violet. "Is that the same thing as lying?"

"Not always," said Jessie. "But sometimes, yes it is."

Suddenly Henry leapt up, the way he always did when he had a big idea. He snapped his fingers. "That's it! I think Dan is lying to Uncle Flick!"

"Lying about what?" Violet asked.

"Lying about keeping the drive-in theater open!" said Jessie. Her eyes got wide. "Yes, it makes perfect sense."

Henry went on. "Dan has been telling Uncle Flick he'll keep running the theater, but really, he doesn't. Because—"

Benny finished for him. "Because he wants to tear it down and make his car store bigger! Just like the lady there said today. Remember?"

Violet repeated the words. " 'We're the biggest place in town to buy a car. And we're getting even bigger.' Oh, no."

The children didn't say anything for a moment. And then Jessie sighed a heavy sigh.

"Maybe we're right about Dan Brinker, but we won't know for sure until it's too late. Because we don't have any proof," she said.

"Why don't we just tell Uncle Flick that we don't trust Dan?" Henry suggested.

Jessie threw up her hands. "Mr. Duke just tried to do the same thing. And look what happened! Uncle Flick got angry." She paced around the kitchen. "If only we could catch him doing something...making trouble at the theater. But I don't think we will."

The others knew what Jessie meant. The theater was closed that day, and all the other pranks had happened on days it was open. There didn't seem to be anything they could do. They all slumped in their chairs. Benny fidgeted and played with a scrap of broken balloon he'd found in his pocket. He stretched it and snapped it with his fingers.

"Benny, where'd you find that?" Jessie asked.

"Behind the screen the other day," said Benny as he stretched and snapped some more.

"That looks like it came off of one of Dan Brinker's cars," Henry pointed out. "It's white, like some of the balloons on his car that very first night. The night he saw the ghost."

"And we figured out there had been a car parked behind the screen," said Jessie. "He must have driven it back there. But why?"

Violet was remembering the thing she'd seen behind the screen the night before. She had forgotten about it until now, and she wondered if it was important. She glanced at Jessie's notebook and at the list they'd made. *Dan Brinker—Wants to sell cars…wants to put ads all over town.* She remembered hearing him on the phone. *I've planned ahead for this deal,* he said. What did that mean?

"You guys?" she said. "We have to go look at something right now."

***

A few minutes later the four children were standing behind the movie screen.

"Jessie, remember that strange bundle you said you saw back here the other day?" Violet asked her sister.

"Yes, but I told you, it's gone now," said Jessie.

Violet pointed upward. "Is that it up there?" she asked.

Jessie looked up, and there, way up along the top of the screen, was something that looked like a very big soft rolled-up blind. It was up so high that it was hard to notice, and

since it was in back of the screen, it couldn't be seen from the theater lot.

"Oh, my gosh, I think it is!" Jessie said. "It's the same color and everything."

Uncle Flick and Grandfather heard the children's voices while they were on their walk. They came behind the screen and joined them. Soon Uncle Flick was peering up at the strange rolled-up thing.

"What on Earth is that? I didn't put that up there!" he said.

"Look, there are cords attached to it," Henry pointed out. "They're tied to the ladders on either side. They must keep it from unrolling."

"Well, why don't we unroll it then, and see what it is?" said Uncle Flick. "Where's Joey? He can help us."

Before long, Henry and Joey were carefully climbing the two metal ladders that ran down the back of the screen. Henry held on tight while he worked to untie the cord and grab it. Joey did the same. Finally they were both holding the cords taut. The rolled-up thing wavered in the wind a little bit, and they could see it was some kind of nylon fabric, the kind used to make parachutes or flags. What was it?

"On the count of three, we'll let go of the cords," shouted Joey. "One, two—three!"

They let go, and the fabric unrolled.

It was an enormous banner, almost as large as the screen! There were words on it:

THE DIAMOND DRIVE-IN IS CLOSED.

COMING SOON—

BRINKER'S AUTO STORE'S EAST LOT!

BIGGER AND BETTER! DRIVE OUT

WITH A DIAMOND DEAL!

The banner had turned the back of the movie screen into a giant billboard that faced the road.

Everyone stared at it in surprise.

"*Closed?* Is that what Dan means to do?" Uncle Flick shouted.

"He's got some nerve," said Grandfather. "To put up that banner even before the place was sold."

"Oh, my goodness," Violet said. "We were right. Dan Brinker really was lying about keeping the drive-in theater open."

Jessie nodded. "He promised the screen would stay standing. Only he wasn't telling the whole truth."

"He's in big trouble!" said Benny. "*That's* the whole truth now."

CHAPTER 10

The Diamond Is Forever

The giant banner on the movie screen could be seen from all around. Cars on the road slowed down to get a better look. A small crowd gathered in front of Duke's Dogs to stare at it. They all wondered about the sign—would the Diamond Drive-In Theater really close down?

"Wait! Stop!" someone called across the road. It was Dan Brinker. He had seen the banner unfurl, too. Now he was hurrying across the road to reach Uncle Flick and the

Aldens. "No, no, it's too early!" he shouted as he reached them. He panted as he tried to catch his breath. "No...nobody was supposed to see that yet!"

"Is that so, Dan?" Uncle Flick said. He glared at Dan. "Just what were you trying to do?"

Dan's forehead was sweaty. He stammered, "I...I had that banner ready so I could display it as soon as the papers were signed! I wanted this theater closed the first chance I got!"

"You were trying to trick me, Dan!" Uncle Flick growled. "You knew I'd never sell this place to you if it meant closing down the theater, so you said you were going to keep it open! But you lied! You weren't even going to wait until the end of the season!"

"And you were the one who caused all the trouble around here!" Joey added bitterly. "Why? We trusted you!"

"I think I know one reason why," Jessie said to Dan. "You had to sneak around the theater to put that banner in place! You brought it over in your car on Thursday night. Then on

Friday you broke Duke's sign so you could climb up the back of the screen!"

"And the ladder made your hands dirty," said Benny. "That's why you didn't take any of my popcorn on Friday night!"

Dan Brinker had lowered his head. "Yes," he said, "You figured it out. I did some of the pranks to create a distraction. And so Flick Fletcher would sell me the place faster."

"You were also trying to make Uncle Flick and Mr. Duke mad at each other, weren't you?" Violet asked.

Dan hung his head even lower. "Yes. That, too. I'm sorry."

Uncle Flick folded his arms. "Dan, you'll have to pay for the damages to the snack bar kitchen. You've done things that are against the law, so I'm going to have to call the police. And, just to be clear, the deal is off!"

"I know," said Dan. "What I did was wrong. All along I knew, deep down, that it was wrong. I should have stopped when I saw the ghost the other night."

"What do you mean?" Jessie asked.

"I know the ghost wasn't real," Dan said.

"But I'll tell you, I was so scared when I saw it! I thought it was some kind of message, telling me I had to stop cheating people, that I had to slow down." He looked thoughtful. "I wish I had."

"Maybe you will now," said Henry. The others nodded in agreement.

Dan Brinker wiped the sweat from his forehead and stood up straight. He walked over to the giant banner. He yanked on one of the corners until the banner came loose and crumpled to the ground. Then he turned and walked back across the road to his store, with his head down.

***

"I'm glad you're not selling the drive-in after all, Flick," said Mr. Duke the next evening. He and Uncle Flick were sitting in lawn chairs in front of the Diamond Drive-In screen. The minivan was parked nearby. The children and Grandfather had decided to stay one more night to see the new movies, *Space Dogs* and *The Rainforest Giant*. Now they were all having a picnic before the movie started. Mr. Duke had bought over food from his stand.

"I'll bet you're glad, Duke," said Uncle Flick. "Especially since I've decided to let my customers bring in your hot dogs."

"They're really good hot dogs," said Jessie as she sat down in a nearby lawn chair. The other Aldens joined her, and soon they were all enjoying the food together.

"I love the onion rings!" said Benny as he picked up a big one and took a bite.

"And don't forget the popcorn from the snack bar," said Violet. "That's good, too."

"Yes, indeed," said Uncle Flick. "We've gotten a new popcorn machine, but we're also going to keep a big shaker of Jessie's popcorn topping on the counter. That is, if you'll give me the recipe."

"Of course!" said Jessie, who smiled proudly.

"I bet Joey and Amy will be happy to be part of the business," Henry said to Uncle Flick.

"I'm making Joey a manager, and Amy will be in charge of special events," Uncle Flick replied. "And now they're planning all kinds of interesting things. In fact, they just borrowed the slide projector. I wonder what they'll use it for."

After a beautiful sunset in the distance behind the screen, it was almost time for the movie to begin. The Aldens took their seats in the minivan. Watch curled up on Jessie's lap. Grandfather turned on the car stereo.

"Here we go," said Henry, as the screen lit up. Then an announcement appeared on the screen:

COMING SOON!

FALL FESTIVAL

AT THE DIAMOND DRIVE-IN THEATER!

HAUNTED HOUSE GALORE!

MOVIES, MYSTERIES, AND MORE!

"Hooray!" Benny shouted as the other children applauded.

"Can we come back next month and go to this, Grandfather?" Violet asked.

"Of course," Grandfather said. "We wouldn't miss it for the world."

"Look!" said Jessie. "There's another announcement!" She pointed to the screen. Now it read:

WE WOULD LIKE TO THANK THE ALDENS—

HENRY, JESSIE, VIOLET, BENNY, AND THEIR

GRANDFATHER—FOR SAVING OUR THEATER.

HONK IF YOU LOVE

THE BOXCAR CHILDREN!

Beep! Beep-beep! Beep! went all the cars in the theater lot. *Beep-beep! Beep!*

"Oh, my goodness!" Violet giggled.

"It sounds like a traffic jam," Henry said, laughing.

"But even better!" said Benny. "Because we can beep back!" Then he reached over and pressed the horn on the minivan. *Beep! Beep! Beep!*

THE BOXCAR CHILDREN

THE RETURN OF THE GRAVEYARD GHOST

Created by
GERTRUDE CHANDLER WARNER

Contents

CHAPTER 1

In the Cemetery

"I think it's going to rain," twelve-year-old Jessie Alden told her younger brother, Benny. "We need to walk faster if we're going to beat the storm," she said. Jessie gently tugged on Watch's leash. The wire-haired terrier trotted between Benny and Jessie, keeping pace with their quick steps.

"I'm going as fast as I can," Benny replied. "The wind keeps pushing me backward." He looked ahead toward his ten-year-old sister, Violet, and fourteen-year-old brother, Henry.

Violet was struggling with the zipper on her jacket and Henry's hat kept flying away in the strong gusts.

"It's too cold," Henry complained as he swooped his hat off the ground for the fifth time and set it firmly over his short brown hair. "Taking Watch for a walk seemed like a good idea an hour ago—"

"It was warmer then," Violet responded with a shiver. Her two high pigtails whipped back in the wind. She gave up on the zipper and wrapped the jacket around her instead. "We should have stayed closer to home." Violet shoved her hands into her pockets.

"Nothing to do about it now," Jessie said as she and Benny caught up with their siblings.

Benny was breathing heavily. "This is crazy strong wind. If you tied a string to me, I'd be a six-year-old kite."

Jessie took Benny's hand in hers and squeezed it tight. "I'll make sure you don't blow away," she said, holding him firmly.

"I have an idea." Henry pointed to the

nearby gate of the Greenfield Cemetery. "There's a shortcut this way."

"Shortcut?" Benny stared past the tall, ornate iron gate toward the moss-covered tombstones. "Sounds good to me. Let's go!" He rushed forward.

"Hang on." Jessie put a hand on Benny's shoulder. "Cemeteries are spooky." Jessie was very brave, but she was also cautious. "Are you *sure* it's okay with you, Benny?"

"I'm not a chicken." Benny put his hands on his hips. "I don't believe in ghosts."

"Once we get to Main Street, we can stop at a shop and call Grandfather for a ride," Henry told them.

"The quicker we get home, the faster we can eat!" At that, Benny's stomach rumbled. "My tummy says it's almost dinner time."

"It's only four o'clock," Henry told Benny after checking his watch.

"Hmmm." Benny pat his belly. "Feels like dinner time. My tummy needs a snack."

"You *always* need a snack!" Henry laughed.

Jessie looked to Violet. Violet often kept quiet about things. Jessie wanted to make sure Violet got a vote before they decided to go through the graveyard.

"Are you scared, Violet?" Jessie asked.

"A little," Violet admitted. "I don't know if I believe in ghosts or not. Sometimes I do. Sometimes I don't..." Violet's voice tapered off. "I suppose if everyone else wants to go that way, it's all right."

"Great!" Benny pushed open the gate. "We all agree. Come on."

Jessie held Watch's leash as they stepped onto the cobblestone path. The sky grew darker with each step they took. Violet moved close to Jessie.

Henry walked ahead with Benny. They were checking out the gravestones, taking turns reading the names and dates out loud.

Greenfield Cemetery was built on a hillside. The wind howled through a thick grove of trees planted in the oldest section. Tombstones in that part dated as far back as the late 1700s.

"There's a lot of history around us," Jessie remarked.

Benny pointed at a tombstone. He sounded out the engraved word. "Soldier."

"The soldier died in 1781. That means he probably fought in the American Revolution," Henry told Benny. "I'll read you a book about the war when we get to the house."

Jessie, Violet, Henry, and Benny lived with their grandfather. After their parents died, they ran away and hid in a railroad boxcar in the woods. They had heard that Grandfather Alden was mean. Even thought they'd never met him, they were afraid. But when he finally found the children, they discovered he wasn't mean at all. Now the children lived with him, and their boxcar was a clubhouse in the backyard.

Watch was the stray dog they'd found on their adventures.

As the first drops of rain began to fall in the cemetery, Watch barked toward a far-off building. It was along another stone pathway past the trees.

"Is that a house?" Benny asked, squinting his eyes. Drops of rain speckled his thick dark-brown hair.

"I think that's the main office," Henry replied, tilting his head to study a squat, brown building. "There's a sign out front. I can't read it, but there's also a parking lot. That's a good clue it's where Mrs. Radcliffe works."

Mrs. Radcliffe was the caretaker of the cemetery. The children had only met her once when they were out with Grandfather. Grandfather Alden had been born in Greenfield and knew practically everyone.

"You're looking the wrong way." Benny tugged on Henry's arm and pointed to the right. He asked again, "I meant is *that* a house?"

Not very far away, tucked among the gravestones, stood a stone structure, much taller than anything else. It was made of white marble, with carved columns and a triangle roof. The building looked like an ancient Greek temple. Several bouquets of white lilies were lying on the front steps.

"It's not a house," Jessie told Benny. "That's called a mausoleum."

"Maus-a-what?" Benny asked.

Violet began to explain. "It's a fancy kind of grave where—" She was about to tell Benny more, when suddenly, lightning flashed. In the glow, the children saw something move by the mausoleum. "Who's that?" Violet asked.

A shadowy figure emerged from behind the building. It was impossible to tell if it was a man or a woman. Whoever it was had on a black jacket with a hood and was moving fast around the tombstones.

The figure stopped and stood near the big mausoleum. An instant later, a flash of lightning zigzagged across the sky and the figure disappeared.

Watch snarled.

Benny stepped back and put a hand on Watch's head. "Watch is scared," he said, leaning in toward the dog. "He thinks we saw a ghost."

Jessie looked at the nervous expression on Benny's face and said, "We should get out of here."

There was a small wall around the back of the mausoleum. They could easily jump over it. Just past that was a café where they could warm up and wait for Grandfather.

Watch barked as the rain began to pour down in heavy sheets. Thunder rattled soon after the lightning.

As the children began to run, Henry glanced back over his shoulder. "Odd," he mumbled, staring at the spot where the cloaked figure had disappeared. "Something strange is going on in Greenfield Cemetery."

CHAPTER 2

The Greenfield Ghost

Randy's Café was packed with people who had also been caught in the rain. Mr. Randy was standing by the front door, handing out towels and helping hang up jackets.

While Violet called Grandfather to let him know where they were, Henry and Benny searched for seats.

Jessie crossed the café to say hello to a girl she knew.

"Hi, Vita." Jessie pointed at the camera in Vita Gupta's hand. "Out taking pictures of the storm?" Vita's nature photos were blue ribbon prizewinners.

"No. I'm changing focus," Vita said. Her short dark hair shook when she giggled at her own pun. "I'm going to make a movie instead of taking pictures. Miss Wolfson asked me to help make a short film about Greenfield using old photographs from the historical society." Vita indicated the older woman at the table and asked Jessie, "Do you know Martha Wolfson?"

"Of course," Jessie said. She turned to Miss Wolfson. "Hello," Jessie greeted her. "Nice to see you again."

"I met Jessie when she came to visit me at the historical society last summer," Miss Wolfson told Vita. She smoothed some loose strands from her gray hair into her bun with one hand. "Jessie interviewed me for a project about old buildings in Greenfield." Looking around, Miss Wolfson asked, "Is Watch with you?" She smiled. "He's a wonderful dog."

"Watch is over there with Benny and Henry." Jessie pointed to her brothers.

"They're looking for a place where we can all sit together. Mr. Randy was very nice to let Watch come into the café during this rainstorm."

"You can join us," Vita said. There were three empty places at the table and something dark on the fourth seat. It was Miss Wolfson's jacket, lying out to dry.

"Hang my jacket on the hook behind you," Miss Wolfson told Jessie. "Then there will be plenty of room for you all." She pointed at an empty spot on the floor near her feet and smiled. "Watch can sit by me. I'll pet him."

Jessie set the jacket on a hook near a large, rain-splattered and steamy window. She waved to get Henry's attention.

Benny came to the table and eyed Miss Wolfson's cookie with a tilted grin.

"Would you like half?" Miss Wolfson asked.

Benny's eyes lit up. "Oh yes, thank you!" he said. He waited patiently as she broke the cookie then ate his half quickly.

Miss Wolfson chuckled and gave Benny the other piece, saying, "Don't spoil your dinner."

"Don't worry," Violet assured her. "Benny's stomach is never full."

Miss Wolfson laughed again.

"Would you like to see a few of the photographs Vita and I have selected for the film so far?" Miss Wolfson brought out a stack of pictures from her purse.

"I love old pictures." Henry leaned in closer.

All the photographs were in black and white. There was one of Greenfield Elementary School, back when it was in a one-room building. There were ten students with a teacher standing in front.

Violet pointed at one of the girls in the picture. "She looks familiar." Violet glanced up at Miss Wolfson. "Is that you?"

Miss Wolfson laughed. "Goodness, no. This was taken before I was born," she told Violet. "But you made a good guess...That's my mom."

"Your mom!" Benny exclaimed. "She's so little."

"She was about your age when this picture was taken," Miss Wolfson told him. She smiled. "Mom's a whole lot older now."

Benny chuckled.

Jessie pointed at another girl about the same age wearing an old-fashioned dress. "Who's that?"

"Patty Wilson," Miss Wolfson said. "She was my mom's best friend." Miss Wolfson pulled out a different picture taken when Patty was in high school. Her blond hair was tucked under a sleek hat and she was wearing a ruffled skirt.

Patty Wilson was standing in front of a dress shop on Main Street. "Patty worked at Madame LaFonte's Dress Shop. It was the fanciest store in town."

Miss Wolfson put that photograph away and showed Violet another one. "This is Greenfield Children's Hospital," she said, "taken right after it opened, almost a hundred years ago."

"I like that picture the best," Vita said. "Did you know Miss Wolfson volunteers at the new hospital building and donates money to families with sick children?" she asked Jessie.

"That's very nice of you," Jessie told Miss Wolfson.

Miss Wolfson said, "It's a worthy cause."

"I think we should put the hospital images on the movie poster," Vita said. "I'd like to print the two pictures side by side; this one from then and a new one to show what the building looks like now. We can sell the posters to help the hospital raise money."

"The hospital always needs money," Miss Wolfson said, considering it. "I do what I can to help, but it's never enough."

"I'll add music to the movie," Vita said. "And we can interview families about the hospital."

While Vita and Miss Wolfson talked about the hospital pictures, Henry handed Jessie another old photograph. This one was of the cemetery's front gate. It was taken so many years earlier hardly any moss was growing on the tombstones. With the sun shining, the cemetery looked like a beautiful park, not a scary place for ghosts to lurk.

"There was someone spooky in the cemetery today." Benny told Miss Wolfson about the figure they'd seen. "They were by the moose-e-lum," he said.

"*Mausoleum*, you mean?" Miss Wolfson asked, raising an eyebrow.

"I don't think it was a ghost," Jessie said. "There were flowers on the steps. I've been thinking that whoever we saw probably was there to leave the bouquets."

"Hmm." Miss Wolfson pressed her lips

together. "The LaFonte family had that monument specially built." She glanced away from Benny toward the window. "But there are no LaFonte family members left in Greenfield. I don't know who might have left flowers—" She paused to consider. "You know, some people say the cemetery is haunted."

"Really?" Violet's eyes widened.

"I don't believe in ghosts," Benny told Miss Wolfson. "Watch was scared though."

"Is that so?" Miss Wolfson asked, glancing down at the terrier.

The door to the café burst open with the wind. A young man wearing a black jacket and hood was standing in the doorway.

After a long look around at the faces in the shop, the boy marched over to Miss Wolfson and introduced himself. "I'm Marcus Michelson," he said. "I'm a new student at the university. Are you Miss Wolfson?"

"I am," she said.

Benny stood and let Marcus have his place. He sat back down, sharing the edge of Violet's seat.

"I think Marcus is the figure we saw in

the cemetery," Henry whispered to Jessie. "He's the right height and he has the right color jacket."

"I'm interested in Greenfield history," Marcus Michelson told Miss Wolfson. He pushed back his coat's hood to reveal short blond hair.

"Is that why you were in the cemetery?" Henry interrupted. Marcus turned to face him. "We saw you standing by the LaFonte mausoleum."

"It couldn't have been me. I never went into the cemetery," Marcus insisted. His green eyes grew wide. "I was outside the gate when I saw a strange figure all dressed in black. I thought it was very suspicious, so I followed—" He looked around the coffee shop. "I was certain whoever it was ducked in here." Marcus shook his head. "I looked around but didn't see anyone who might fit the description. Then I noticed Miss Wolfson." He caught her eye and said, "I've been meaning to call you."

"How can I help you?" Mrs. Wolfson asked.

"Well, I—" Marcus began when suddenly the lights in the coffee shop flickered off. The room plunged into darkness.

Watch jumped onto Jessie's lap.

Benny gave Violet a hug and whispered, "Don't worry. I'll protect you."

"I'll protect you too," Violet said, hugging him back.

When the lights came back on a few moments later, a woman screamed.

Her husband, pale and shaken, pointed to the window behind Henry's head.

A single lily lay across the windowsill. The raindrops on the window glittered on the glass, making the flower shine eerily.

Vita pressed a button on her camera. "Scoot over, please, Jessie," she said, holding the lens to her eye. "I want to record this."

"What's going on?" Jessie asked Miss Wolfson.

Miss Wolfson stared at the flower. She studied the frightened faces of the people in the café. Then she looked directly into the lens of Vita's camera and announced, "The LaFonte ghost has returned."

CHAPTER 3

The LaFonte Mausoleum

"Who's the LaFonte ghost?" Henry asked Miss Wolfson.

"A g-g-ghost?" Benny asked. "There's a real ghost in Greenfield?"

"I thought you didn't believe in ghosts," Jessie said.

Benny raised his shoulders. "That was before we saw something in the cemetery and the lights went out and...that!" He pointed at the flower. "I've changed my mind." Benny shivered and whispered in Watch's ear,

"Ghosts. Yikes."

People in the café gathered around Miss Wolfson as she began to share a bit of history.

"Today is the seventy-fifth anniversary of the death of Madame Jacqueline LaFonte," she told the crowd.

"She was the dressmaker." Jessie picked up the historic photograph of the LaFonte shop on Main Street.

"Yes." Miss Wolfson went on, saying, "Women would come to have dresses made, then stay for tea and conversation." With a small smile she added, "Madame LaFonte was known to give very good advice. Some people even say Jacqueline was a fortune-teller."

"Very interesting," Jessie said, setting the photo on the table and taking a notebook out of her small purse. Jessie wrote down Madame Jacqueline LaFonte's name as a reminder to see if she could find any information about her online. Jessie liked to research interesting people.

"Ever since the first anniversary of her death, people in Greenfield have believed that Jacqueline LaFonte's ghost haunts the cemetery," Miss Wolfson said.

"Ooh," Vita said, recording the café conversation. "A ghost story is way more interesting than a historical society film." She stood on a chair to get a good view of the room through her camera. She focused her lens on the most frightened expressions.

The door to the café opened and Grandfather Alden walked in. "Looks like I'm interrupting an important meeting," he remarked as he

closed his umbrella. He walked over to Henry and asked, "What's going on?"

Henry pointed to the windowsill.

"Ah," Grandfather said, stepping over to Miss Wolfson. "It's the three-day warning?"

The historian nodded.

At Jessie's questioning look, Grandfather explained, "Every year around Halloween, white lilies are placed on the LaFonte grave. After that, a lily appears somewhere in town. It's said that lilies were Jacqueline LaFonte's favorite flower. But some people also believe that lilies are a symbol of death." Grandfather said.

He continued. "After the flower shows up, everyone has three days to bring gifts to the LaFonte mausoleum. Those who leave gifts get a year of good fortune. Those who ignore the warning receive nothing but bad luck all year."

Miss Wolfson clarified. "Gifts can be food, silver, money, jewelry—anything to make Jacqueline's ghost happy."

Benny got up and moved to stand near Grandfather. There were goose bumps along his arms. "I like gifts," he said in a shaky voice.

"So does the ghost," Miss Wolfson told Benny.

"Nonsense," Grandfather Alden cut in. "I've known this ghost story my whole life. There's no LaFonte ghost. Bad things happen to people sometimes—that's just the way life is. Good things happen too. It doesn't matter whether or not someone leaves presents in the cemetery."

"You're wrong. The ghost is real." A well-dressed woman in the back of the room stood up. She looked directly at Grandfather and asked, "Ever hear of Patricia Wilson? Patty didn't heed the warning, never left a gift, and she...disappeared!"

Several people in the room gasped.

"That's an old made-up rumor from the year after Jacqueline's death," Mr. Randy said from behind the cash register. "Patricia Wilson didn't disappear. My mother was a child back then and knew her."

Miss Wolfson pointed out Mr. Randy's mother in the photo taken in front of the old school house, a girl who looked to be about Violet's age.

"Mama knew Patty," Mr. Randy said in a booming voice that filled the café. "She told me that Patty left town on her own."

The woman turned to face Mr. Randy. "Believe what you want," she said, gathering her coat and scarf. "I won't risk having a year of bad luck. I'm going to put a gift at the cemetery tomorrow."

"What do you think?" Henry asked Jessie as people in the café began to discuss whether or not they were going to set out gifts for the ghost.

Jessie looked down at her notebook where she'd written Jacqueline LaFonte's name. On the next line, she wrote Patricia Wilson. And below that she drew a giant question mark.

"I'd like to learn more about the ghost," Jessie replied.

"And the gifts," Benny chimed in.

"We should go back to the cemetery," Henry suggested as a streak of lightning flashed across the sky outside the café.

"Can we go tomorrow?" Benny asked, patting his belly. "Now it really is dinner-time, and I'm starved! I'm extra brave when my tummy's full." He shivered again. "Ghosts. Yikes."

"The cemetery won't be so creepy in the daylight," Violet agreed.

Henry looked at the white lily and its reflection in the window glass. "We'll start ghost hunting tomorrow morning," he said.

Jessie quickly peeked over at Benny and added, "Right after breakfast."

"Perfect!" Benny grinned as they followed Grandfather to the car for the ride home.

CHAPTER 4

Gifts for Ghosts

"Isn't that Marcus Michelson?" Violet pointed toward the cemetery gate. She was walking with Jessie and her brothers. Marcus was coming straight toward them.

Jessie checked the time. They'd left home just after breakfast as planned. "He's out early," she remarked. "I wonder what he's doing here."

It wasn't raining anymore, but it was still cold. Marcus was wearing the same dark jacket as the evening before, but now his hood was down. In his hands he carried a cardboard box.

Benny was holding Watch's leash. When Watch saw Marcus, he tugged forward, pulling out of Benny's hand and running down the sidewalk.

Marcus wasn't paying attention and stumbled backward when Watch jumped up to greet him.

"Whoa!" Marcus said, dropping the box as Watch's leash tangled around his ankles. The lid on the box popped open and the contents spilled out. Two silver candlesticks lay on the sidewalk.

Henry rushed after the dog. "Sorry," he told Marcus.

"Watch just wants to make a new friend," Benny said. "He's a happy dog."

Henry unwound the leash then handed the end to Jessie.

"Are you all right?" Violet asked. Marcus seemed distracted. His eyes were darting around the area, not focusing on any one thing.

"I'm fine. I have to go." Marcus collected

the candlesticks and set them carefully back into the box. "Now we'll see," he muttered to himself and then, without another word to the Aldens, he stomped through the cemetery gates.

Jessie watched him go.

"I think we should follow him," Henry suggested. "It looks like he's going to the LaFonte mausoleum."

"Do you think the candlesticks are a gift for the ghost?" Benny asked. "Do you think we should leave a gift too?"

"Grandfather said it's all made up," Henry reminded Benny. "No such thing as the LaFonte ghost."

"Lots of people believe the ghost is real." Benny lowered his voice and added, "And Patty Wilson disappeared..."

"She might have just left town," Jessie said.

"I agree with Benny," Violet admitted. "Until we know for sure what happened to Patty Wilson, I think we should leave a gift too."

"When we get home, I'll find a nice present for the ghost. Just in case she's real," Benny told Violet. "We don't want any bad luck."

The children entered the cemetery and stayed hidden in a grove of trees near the mausoleum. They watched as Marcus set down his box and removed the candlesticks. He carefully arranged them near a column then picked up the empty box and walked away.

"What do you think is going to happen to Marcus's gift?" Violet asked Henry.

"I think someone will come and get it," Henry replied. "Then we will know who is pretending to be the ghost."

"Isn't that stealing?" Jessie asked. "I mean, if someone invented a ghost to scare people into leaving food and silver and jewelry, then sneak in and collect it all—that seems like stealing to me."

"Right," Henry agreed. "The person who is doing this is definitely a thief."

"It's a ghost," Benny argued. "Not a thief."

"Where would the ghost put all those presents?" Henry asked.

"The ghost makes them magically disappear," Benny said.

"Magically disappear to where?" Henry pressed Benny to think about his answer.

"People have been leaving things for the LaFonte ghost for seventy-four years. That's a lot of gifts."

"Not too many," Benny replied. "If I got presents on my birthday and at Christmas every year, I'd never run out of places to put all my gifts," Benny said. "They could all fit in the toy box and under the bed and in the closet." He smiled. "I have plenty of room for a hundred years of presents."

"You're funny," Henry said. "But ghosts don't have beds and closets. I think we need to stay here all day to see who's taking the gifts and prove there is no ghost."

"Maybe we can find out where the thief is putting the presents and return them to their owners," Jessie suggested.

"If we catch a person pretending to be a ghost, I *won't* believe in ghosts," Violet said very practically. "And if we see a real ghost, then I *will* believe in them."

"Ghosts. Yikes," Benny said as they searched for a better place to hide.

Jessie and Violet found a good spot in the old grove of trees where they could keep an

eye on Marcus's candlesticks. Benny climbed up one of the trees for a better view.

Since they were going to be there all day, Henry ran home to take Watch back and pick up a pair of binoculars. He returned right away.

Hours later, Violet was bored. Besides Marcus, no one else had come to leave gifts at the mausoleum and Marcus's candlesticks were still sitting there. "I am beginning to think there's no ghost *and* no thief," she said. "Nothing interesting is going on."

"I'm cold," Jessie said. She'd left her hat at home and forgotten to ask Henry to pick it up when he went back.

Violet sneezed. "I'm cold too."

"And I'm hungry," Benny called down from the tree branch where he was camped out.

"I brought you lunch," Henry said, looking up at his brother.

"But that was *hours* ago," Benny said.

"And I brought snacks." Henry pointed at a trash bag filled with empty granola bar wrappers.

"We ran out ten minutes ago," Benny said with a sigh. "I ate them all."

"Hang in there," Henry told his siblings. "We can't give up yet. Something is going to happen—" Just then, he saw movement near the mausoleum. Henry put the binoculars to his eyes and adjusted the focus.

"What do you see?" Benny asked, sitting up straight and leaning forward. "Is it the ghost?"

"Or a person?" Jessie squinted in the direction Henry was looking.

Henry said, "I saw someone behind a tree. But just his or her arm—a black coat sleeve. Then it disappeared."

"A ghost," Benny said surely.

"A person," Jessie said, also certain.

Violet didn't take a side. She sneezed again instead.

"Get out!" A spooky voice called through the trees.

"Ghost!" Benny leapt down from the tree, knocking down Jessie.

"Person," Jessie said, getting up and turning him around to face Mrs. Radcliffe, the graveyard caretaker.

"Leave!" Mrs. Radcliffe pointed her long bony finger to the exit gate. "You are not welcome in my cemetery." Hunched over, wearing a black cloak, Mrs. Radcliffe looked like the wicked witch in the Hansel and Gretel story.

"We're watching for the LaFonte ghost," Henry said. "We're going to prove she's fake."

Mrs. Radcliffe shook her head. "Ghosts are supposed to scare people..." She muttered, "I've already chased someone else away. Now you all need to go too."

"Someone was hiding in the cemetery?" Violet asked. "Who?"

"I wish you'd all go away!" Mrs. Radcliffe said. "Everyone is leaving trash around, trampling on my grass, stepping on the flowers..." She didn't answer Violet's question. "I have to clean up. More work for me."

She led them to the gate and warned, "Stay outside the cemetery. I don't want you traipsing all over the place and climbing my trees! Leave my ghosts alone!"

"Ghosts?" Violet asked after Mrs. Radcliffe was gone. "Like more than one?"

"I don't think she really means that the cemetery is full of ghosts," Jessie said. "I think she's just trying to scare us away."

"It worked. I don't want to go back to the cemetery ever!" Benny gritted his teeth. "That lady is scarier than a ghost!"

"She's scary for sure," Violet agreed. "But how are we going to find out if there's a ghost *or* a thief without going back into the cemetery?"

Henry pointed to a tree outside the property. "Benny, can you climb up there and see if the candlesticks are still at the mausoleum?" he asked. Then to Violet, "Maybe we can investigate from here."

"I feel safer out here." Benny quickly climbed the tree and surveyed the graveyard with Henry's binoculars. "Uh-oh. There's trouble," he reported. "You know how Marcus was the only one who left a gift today?"

"Yes," Jessie said, encouraging him to go on.

"Well, people must have been waiting till they were done with work—" Benny slid down the tree trunk. "Lots and lots of people are coming toward the cemetery now. And they're all carrying boxes."

Violet looked past Benny with the binoculars. "I see Vita. She's hiding in the bushes with her video camera." She handed the binoculars to Henry, saying, "If Mrs. Radcliffe spots her, she'll be chased out here with us."

Jessie shook her head. "Mrs. Radcliffe will never be able to chase everyone out of the cemetery."

"Let me see." Henry climbed up the tree to the branch where Benny had been. "There are a lot of people. I see Vita. There's the mausoleum. And—"

He put down the binoculars with a surprised look on his face.

"Marcus Michelson's candlesticks are gone!"

CHAPTER 5

Spooky Suspects and Creepy Clues

"How about this?" Benny held up one of Jessie's dolls from the toy bin in the boxcar clubhouse. She was dirty, had matted hair and a missing an arm, and wore only one shoe.

"I don't think you should give Beautiful Betsy to the ghost." Violet frowned. "She's not so beautiful anymore. That doll looks like she's had a lot of bad luck."

"There was no bad luck. Betsy was my favorite." Jessie defended her doll. "Grandfather gave her to me when we first came to live here. I used to take her everywhere with me."

"Still...Violet's right," Benny said with a frown. "The ghost would want something nicer." Benny put Betsy back in the toy box and searched around for something else. "How about this?" He held up one of Henry's old baseball gloves. It smelled bad. "Maybe not," he said, plugging his nose and tossing the glove back in the bin.

"You're not going to need a gift," Jessie assured Benny. "There's no ghost."

Jessie was at her desk, staring at the computer screen as a web page loaded.

Henry was standing over her shoulder. "There," he said. "Click on Jacqueline LaFonte's name." He scanned the source. "This is what the local newspaper said about her after she died."

Jessie read the page silently to herself then described what it said. "The whole article is about how Jacqueline was a kind woman who loved Greenfield." Jessie pinched her lips together. "I don't think Jacqueline LaFonte would haunt this town.

It says here that she gave a lot of money to charity."

"Nice ghosts can be scary," Benny said.

"Jacqueline gave her money away," Henry said. "She didn't take anything from others." He glanced at the shiny plastic bead necklaces Benny was now holding. "It doesn't sound like she was the kind of person who'd want other people's jewelry and candlesticks."

"Then why do people leave gifts for her?" Violet asked. "There must be a reason."

"I don't know how it started," Jessie said as she flipped through a few more web sites. "I can't find anything about the beginning, but it says here that after her death people avoided her family because of the bad luck rumors. No one went to their businesses. The dress shop had to close. People were scared of the ghost and that made them scared of the LaFontes." She shook her head. "The family was run out of town. It's a shame."

Henry was using the Internet on his cell phone to help Jessie find out more information. "Hey, look here," he said, turning the phone screen around toward the others. "There's an old house on the hill behind the cemetery. It used to be their family home. No one's lived there for a long time. It's all run down now." Henry marked the web site photo. "We should check it out."

"I'll need a whole lot of snacks if I'm going to be brave enough to visit an abandoned house," Benny said, stretching as far as he could into the toy bin.

Violet gave him a playful push. Benny fell forward, toppling into the box. He was laughing as he dug himself out. "Maybe I should share my snacks with the ghost instead of giving her our old toys." He quickly changed his mind. "Nah." Benny ducked back into the bin. "I want the food. The ghost can have some toys."

Jessie opened her notebook and wrote a note to visit the old LaFonte house. Then she turned to a fresh page.

"Let's imagine we are catching a gift thief," she said. "Who are the suspects?"

"The ghost," Benny's muffled voice came from the bottom of the toy chest. "The ghost is the first suspect."

Jessie didn't argue. She wrote it down.

"Marcus Michelson." Violet said. "He's new to town and has a black coat. We've seen him near the cemetery a couple times, which means he could be the one stealing the gifts. When we saw him at the café, he looked just like the spooky figure we'd seen near the mausoleum."

Jessie wrote his name down, along with all of Violet's reasons.

"But we also saw him putting his own gift out for the ghost," Henry said.

"Maybe I'm wrong," Violet admitted. "Until we know more, he should be a suspect."

"Okay. Let's find out what we can about Marcus," Jessie said, turning in her chair. She was rubbing her chin. Jessie did that when she was thinking really hard. "He could easily have set the flower on the café window."

Benny popped up. "That means the ghost was in the café! Yikes."

"The person *pretending* to be the ghost was in the café," Henry corrected. He nodded toward Jessie's list. "Marcus Michelson is a suspect. But then, so is Miss Wolfson."

Jessie wrote down the historian's name, saying, "She was closest to the window when the lights went out. She had a black coat hanging on a hook. And it was wet. And she knows the most about the LaFonte ghost."

"Put Mrs. Radcliffe on the list too," Benny said, crawling out of the toy box with a handful of possible gifts.

"But she wasn't in the café," Violet argued.

"It doesn't matter if she was there or not. I think she's creepy," Benny replied, shaking his head.

"That's not a good reason to think someone is a thief," Henry said. "We can't just put her on the list because she looks like a witch and yells at children—"

"What if..." Jessie interrupted. "What if Mrs. Radcliffe invented the ghost to keep people out of the cemetery?"

"Her cloak *is* black," Violet said.

"She could have turned off the café lights, sneaked in, placed the flower, and left before anyone noticed," Henry added.

"If she wants to scare people away, her plan's not working," Benny said, reminding them of the big crowd that was going to the cemetery with gifts.

"Let's put her on the suspect list," Henry told Jessie. "Just in case."

"Okay." Jessie wrote down Mrs. Radcliffe's name. "We have three possible gift-stealing thieves."

"And one ghost," Benny added. "Don't forget there is still the possibility the ghost is real."

"Right." Jessie checked the list. "Anyone else to consider?"

The room fell silent as everyone thought about who they'd seen lurking around the cemetery.

"Vita, maybe," Violet said. "Maybe she invented the ghost. She decided really fast to make a movie about it. An exciting scary movie could make her famous, right?"

"It's possible," Jessie said. "And she was inside the café—"

"Wait!" Henry suddenly interrupted. "We have a problem." He breathed a heavy sigh and said, "A big problem."

"What?" everyone asked at the same time.

"The ghost was first spotted a year after Madame LaFonte died," Henry said. "That means whoever has been taking the gifts from the cemetery has been doing it for seventy-four years! No one on our list is old enough to have been there at the beginning."

"Oh." Jessie leaned back in her chair. "That is a problem," she admitted.

"A big problem," Violet echoed, tapping her foot.

"There's only one answer then." Benny found a roll of wrapping paper and began to wrap the toys he'd selected. "The LaFonte ghost is real!" He shuddered and added, "Yikes!"

CHAPTER 6

Patty Wilson

"We need to talk to the people on our suspect list," Jessie said.

Henry agreed. "Even though no one has been around for more than seventy-four years, maybe one of them still holds a clue to this ghost-thief mystery."

He called Vita Gupta.

Vita told him that she was headed to the cemetery to film Miss Wolfson talking about the legend of Jacqueline's ghost. Vita said they could meet there.

"I couldn't sleep last night," Jessie told the others as they walked to the cemetery.

"What did you do?" Benny asked. "Read? Watch TV? Din-eakfast?" He grinned at his new word. "That's the meal between dinner and breakfast."

"None of those," Jessie said with a small giggle. "I went to the boxcar and did some research. I found out what happened to Patty Wilson."

"Really?" Violet stepped up next to Jessie. "What'd you learn? I'm curious."

"So did she leave town on her own?" Henry asked. He dropped his voice to a spooky growl. "Or did the ghost get her?" Sneaking behind Violet, he tapped her on the shoulder.

"Augh!" Violet jumped.

They all laughed.

"This whole ghost thing still scares me a little," Violet admitted.

"And me a lot," Benny said, reaching into his jeans pocket. He pulled out a squished granola bar in a crinkled plastic bag. "Want a snack for bravery?" He held the bar out to Violet.

"No, thanks," she said, eyeing the flattened honey-coated nut mixture.

"I'll eat it then." Benny peeled a piece of the bar away from the plastic. He tapped his other pocket. "I have another one in case I get scared later." Benny looked at Violet. "You can share it if you feel nervous."

Violet ruffled his brown hair and winked. "You're a good little brother."

Changing the subject back to Jessie's research, Henry asked, "What did you find out?"

Jessie handed Henry a page she'd printed from the Internet. It was an old newspaper article.

"Patty's sister was sick. She left town to help the family," Jessie said as Benny tugged hard on the cemetery gate to open it. "In those days, small newspapers used to run brief news articles about people in town. I'm guessing that no one thought to search other towns around Greenfield for information about her. I checked old newspaper records and found something from the town of Beacon Crest."

"I've never heard of Beacon Crest," Henry said.

"It doesn't exist now," Jessie told him. "When Silver Spring grew bigger, Beacon Crest became part of it. But seventy-five years ago, it was its own town."

"Clever, Jessie," Violet complimented her.

Jessie smiled. "Thanks."

Henry read the short newspaper notice out loud: "*Mrs. Laura Thompson was visited this week by her sister, Miss Patricia Wilson of Greenfield. Mrs. Thompson is at home, resting from her illness.*

"I knew it," Henry said as he led the way toward the mausoleum. "No ghostly bad luck."

"Or maybe it was the ghost's bad luck that got her sister sick," Benny suggested. "I mean, if she didn't leave Jacqueline LaFonte a gift, it's possible."

"Good point." Henry shrugged. "I guess I'm going to have to work harder to show you that the ghost doesn't exist."

"Try your best," Benny said. "Until you prove it to me, I'm going to eat granola bars. Just in case you're wrong."

Violet wrapped her clean fingers around Benny's sticky ones. "We're protecting each other," she said with a wink.

"Yes, we are," Benny replied.

There was a big crowd at the LaFonte mausoleum. Miss Wolfson was in the center of the group, standing on a small step stool, talking in a loud voice.

"It all began one year after Jacqueline LaFonte died…" Miss Wolfson was saying.

"Looks like we didn't miss much," Henry whispered.

Marcus Michelson was near the front, hands in his black jacket pockets, listening intently.

Vita was there too. Her camera scanned the crowd and then focused on Miss Wolfson.

The Aldens stayed near the back of the crowd to listen.

"On the first anniversary of Madame LaFonte's death, Patricia Wilson found a lily near the LaFonte dress shop window. Frightened, Patty ran down the street and found my mother at the bakery, working behind the counter. Patty was the assistant to

Jacqueline at the dress shop. Patty said that before she died, Jacqueline announced that she planned to 'return' on her anniversary and that people should bring gifts to her grave or she'd bring bad luck."

A man near Marcus put his arm around his wife. She was holding a bouquet of flowers and a box of chocolates. Together they stepped forward and set the items on the steps of the mausoleum.

"My mother immediately left a gift. Patty meant to, she said she would, but she forgot." Miss Wolfson squinted her eyes and peered slowly across the faces of the audience. "Patricia Wilson disappeared before the three days passed."

"That's not exactly true," Jessie blurted out. All eyes turned to face her. She blushed. "Sorry. I didn't mean to interrupt," Jessie told Miss Wolfson. She reached into her coat pocket and took out the article. "Last night I discovered that Patty Wilson had been visiting her sick sister." She held up the page. "Exactly seventy-four years ago this time of year. Which means she left on her own. It wasn't a ghost that got her. She didn't really disappear."

Vita turned her camera on the Aldens.

Henry stood tall and said, "Maybe Patricia Wilson didn't tell anyone she was leaving. We think it was an emergency. Then she probably stayed in Beacon Crest and didn't come back."

"Look. There's more." Jessie held up a second sheet of paper and said, "I found more newspaper items about Patricia. She married and became Patricia Haverford and then she died in Silver City. Here's her death notice. Patty Wilson lived to be ninety-two years old. She had children and grandchildren."

People began to mutter and whisper to each other. It was as if no one had listened to Jessie.

"I heard about a man whose business went bankrupt," a lady reported. "And a girl who broke her arm."

"Well, I heard about a boy who got food poisoning. And one time, a man didn't leave a gift and a big storm came. A tree fell on the man's car."

Everyone had a bad luck story to tell about what had happened to someone who hadn't left Jacqueline LaFonte's ghost a present.

"That's all normal stuff," Henry said in a loud voice. "Bad stuff happens to everyone, but so does good stuff." That was exactly what Grandfather had told the children at the café when they saw the lily appear.

"It's the ghost's curse," someone said from deep inside the crowd.

Violet stood on her tiptoes but couldn't see who said it.

A nervous hush came over the people at the mausoleum. A little boy quickly walked to the pillars and set down a box of crayons near the name plaque. Three young girls put down home baked treats. A man set out candles and a woman carefully set down a pretty potted plant.

As the gifts piled up, Jessie turned to Henry, Violet, and Benny. She waved the articles. "I don't understand," she said. "I have proof that Patricia Wilson didn't disappear, but no one believes it."

Henry frowned. "Let's go talk to Miss

Wolfson. She's a historian. She has to believe the facts."

Because he was the smallest, Benny got through the crowd first.

Miss Wolfson was talking to Marcus Michelson. Vita was recording their conversation.

"I've changed my mind," Vita was telling Miss Wolfson. "Instead of the historical society film, I'm making a ghost documentary," Vita said. "I'm going to show the entire town coming out to leave gifts for the ghost. I've already talked to a big-time producer about making a spooky cemetery movie. She thinks I might become a famous director."

Miss Wolfson smiled and waved to the camera. "Hello, Hollywood," she said with a grin. Then Miss Wolfson sneezed. "Excuse me," she told Vita. "I think I might be getting a cold."

Violet reached forward and handed Miss Wolfson a tissue. "Me too," she said with a sneeze.

Miss Wolfson took the tissue. "Thank

you," she said. Then turned, "Jessie, can I see your pages?"

Jessie handed her the pages. Miss Wolfson took a quick glance before handing them back. "Good luck," she told Jessie.

"With what?" Violet asked. Miss Wolfson was acting strange.

"With convincing people that there is no ghost," Miss Wolfson said, putting her hands on her hips. "People believe what they want to believe. Remember my mom in the old school picture? Now, she's ninety-five years old. Just yesterday, she told me that even if Patty Wilson herself walked into the cemetery right now and declared she hadn't been cursed, no one would believe her. The ghost and the gifts and the story about bad luck are part of Greenfield's history. *Nothing* you do will change that." She added, "We all might as well make the best of it."

Bending down, Miss Wolfson told Benny, "Bring some toys. I'm sure the ghost would especially like to have a few stuffed animals and some board games."

Marcus Michelson's face became very red.

"It's time for people to know the truth." He stomped his foot, then put the hood of his black coat over his head and shouted at Mrs. Wolfson, "For all the trouble that ghost has caused, those gifts should be mine!" With that, Marcus stormed out of the cemetery.

He left just in time because a few minutes later Mrs. Radcliffe appeared. She was carrying a broom and swinging it like a weapon. "Get out," she shrieked, sweeping at people's feet. "Out of my cemetery. Stay off the grass. Don't trample the flowers." People moved aside, but no one left. Finally in frustration, Mrs. Radcliffe muttered, "The LaFonte ghost isn't scary enough to keep people away. This cemetery needs a zombie!" With an angry huff, she stomped back to her office.

CHAPTER 7

Movie Magic

"Is there a zombie in Greenfield?" Benny asked at breakfast the next morning. "Mrs. Radcliffe said the cemetery needed a zombie." The children were sitting at the dining room table, which was laid out with bowls and spoons.

Violet came in from the kitchen carrying a box of cereal and a carton of milk. "Mrs. Radcliffe is just trying to frighten people away from the cemetery," Violet told Benny. "Ghosts maybe. Zombies...no way."

"A zombie would be scarier than a ghost," Benny said while pouring a bowl of crunchy flakes. "But know what would be even scarier?"

"What?" Jessie asked.

"Grrr," Benny snarled, showing his teeth. "A werewolf."

Jessie laughed. "Or a vampire." She covered her neck with two hands. "That would scare me."

"Mrs. Radcliffe scares me," Henry said with a wink. "I think she can chase people away from the cemetery all on her own!"

Everyone agreed.

"Good morning," Grandfather greeted the children as he brought his coffee cup and joined them at the table. "How's the ghost hunt going?"

"After last night, our suspects are all now more suspicious," Henry replied.

"It's day three," Jessie said. "The last day for people to bring gifts to the mausoleum."

"Or get bad luck." Benny trembled. "A whole year of bad luck."

Violet said to Grandfather, "If we don't find a person acting like the ghost today, we might have to admit that the ghost is real."

"Or wait till next year to search around again," Henry said, shaking his head.

"So what's your plan for today?" Grandfather Alden asked as they finished their cereal. "Are you going back to the cemetery?"

"Maybe we should hide again and see if we can catch the person gathering the gifts," Henry suggested.

Jessie opened her notebook. "Remember when Henry found out about the old LaFonte house on the hill? I think we should go there," she said. "Maybe we can find a clue in the house."

Benny took his empty bowl and got up to go into the kitchen. "I'm going to need a lot of snacks if we're visiting a spooky haunted house." He patted his empty pockets. "Lots and lots of snacks."

"That reminds me," Jessie said, getting up from the table, "Watch is probably hungry too." She called to the dog. "Watch! Come here, Watch!"

Usually Watch came running at the sound of Jessie's voice. But not today.

"Watch!" she called again.

"Where's that dog?" Henry asked, going to search the bedrooms. "I bet he's sleeping, or—"

Just then Benny came running in from the kitchen. "Watch is gone!"

"What do you mean?" Violet asked, hurrying to Benny's side. She looked worried.

"When I came downstairs this morning, Watch wanted to go outside. So I tied his leash to the patio table. Now Watch is gone." Benny's eyes were wide. "I knew it! We should have brought a gift to the mass-o-lume."

"Mausoleum," Jessie corrected as she came back into the dining room. "There's no ghost."

"Then how do you explain this?" Benny held up Watch's leash. "Watch escaped. We have bad luck! We have bad, bad luck!"

Benny ran from the room and came back a second later, still in his pajamas and his morning hair sticking up to the sky. He was holding a big bag of toys. "Gifts for the ghost. We have to deliver them right now so Watch will come back. Hurry, Jessie. Hustle, Henry. Come on, Violet." He slipped on his tennis shoes. "Let's go to the..." he said it slowly to be sure he said it right, "...mausoleum."

***

Watch wasn't at the cemetery. But plenty of people were there, and the area around the LaFonte mausoleum was piled high with gifts.

Benny walked carefully through the crowd until he reached one of the columns. He set down his bag of toys and began to put them on the ground one at a time near the mausoleum steps.

"Wait!" Vita rushed to him. "Can you take them back and do it again? I want to record you for my movie."

Benny waited for his siblings to catch up. He asked Henry, "Is it bad luck to take them back? We've had enough bad luck already."

"I think it's all right," Henry assured Benny. "You really don't have to give gifts at all."

"Yes, we do! We have to save our dog!" Glancing down at his pajama bottoms, Benny told Vita, "We're kind of in a hurry to get these presents to the ghost." He asked, "Have you seen Watch? He's missing."

"That's terrible!" Vita said. "How about this? After I record you putting out the gifts, I'll help you find your dog. Filming will only take a couple minutes."

Benny agreed and took back his presents, putting them into the bag.

Vita asked him to move into the crowd while she framed the shot. She wanted the old grove of trees behind him and the LaFonte house on the hill in the distance. Looking through her lens, Vita shouted, "Action!"

Benny wove his way through the people

around the mausoleum toward the column again. He took the gifts out one by one and set them down. He had ten different wrapped packages. Then Benny turned to Vita's camera and said, "We don't want any bad luck. We just want our dog back."

Vita put down the lens. "That was perfect," she told Benny. "I'll quickly review it to make sure I got everything and that it's in focus. Then we can search for Watch."

Benny said, "I'm worried about our dog. Thanks for helping us."

"Thanks to you too," Vita replied. She switched the camera into playback mode.

"Did you know about the ghost story before you decided to make the movie?" Jessie asked Vita.

"No," Vita said. "I found out the same way you did. The lights went out at Randy's Café and then the lily appeared. That was the beginning." She looked at the small screen on her camera and rewound the part she'd filmed with Benny.

Violet took Jessie aside. "It doesn't sound like Vita is a suspect anymore."

"She didn't make up the ghost for her movie," Jessie agreed, taking out her notebook and crossing off Vita's name. "It was a coincidence that she was at the café that night."

Jessie closed the notebook and everyone huddled around Vita's camera to see the bit with Benny.

There he was, standing in the crowd. Then she moved out to the trees.

"Wait till I add spooky music," Vita said. "This is going to be awesome!"

From the trees, her lens panned up to the old house on the hill and then down to focus on Benny...

Suddenly, Vita gasped. She pressed the stop button on the camera and then pushed the footage back a few frames.

"What do you see?" Henry asked.

"Is it the ghost?" Benny shivered.

She zoomed in toward the house. "Look at this." Vita turned the tiny screen toward Henry and Jessie. Violet and Benny squeezed in to see. "There's something moving. There—" Vita's eyes went wide. "Near the front porch. By the steps."

"That's not a ghost!" Jessie gasped. She jumped up and started to run toward the house on the hill. "It's Watch!"

CHAPTER 8

Haunted House

"Don't worry." Benny untied the cord that held Watch to the splintered wooden stake in front of the LaFonte house. "We gave the ghost presents. Lots of presents. No more bad luck for the Aldens!"

"Watch didn't run away," Henry said, hooking Watch's leash to his collar. "Someone took him. On purpose."

"I wonder why," Jessie said, bending down to hug her dog. "Is someone trying to scare us away?"

Violet looked up at the old house and wrinkled her forehead. "Maybe whoever is pretending to be the ghost wanted us to come here."

"I don't think anyone wanted us to come here," Benny said. "In fact, I think we should leave. Fast as we can."

The LaFonte house was dark and dusty. When a gust of wind blew, the enormous house swayed. It was hard to imagine what it had been like when Jacqueline LaFonte lived there. It must have been beautiful, but now the windows were all broken. The fence had toppled down and was rotten. The garden was a field of weeds.

Jessie saw a rat scurry under the porch.

Violet glanced over her shoulder. "I want to go inside," she said.

"Come on, Violet." Vita was right behind her, camera held high. "We have a mystery to solve." She added, "This is going to be the best movie ever."

The children entered through a side door with broken hinges. The door led into a small kitchen area, where rusted appliances sat covered with silken spider webs and thick dust.

"I don't like it in here," Benny said, squeezing himself between Henry and Jessie. Benny took a granola bar out of his pocket but didn't eat it. He held it in his hand to give him courage.

The living room was in better shape than the kitchen, but barely. Antique furniture had been covered with sheets. The chandeliers were black with tarnish. The ceiling beams appeared sturdy, but birds had nested in the wide cracks.

"Okay," Violet said with a quick look around. "Nothing to see. No clues to who might be pretending to be a ghost." She crossed her arms and hugged herself. "No gifts. Let's go."

Henry insisted they take a peek in the dining room and a small parlor across the hall before they could leave. "No one would be foolish enough to try those stairs." He indicated that the only way to the second floor was a narrow stairway with wilted boards and a broken handrail.

"A dead end. This is disappointing," Jessie said. "I hoped that the answer to who was playing the LaFonte ghost and what was happening to the gifts would be in this old house."

Henry headed to the front door. "We can leave this way." Reaching out, Henry said, "I'll unlock—"

The knob rattled.

"It's the ghost!" Benny exclaimed. "Yikes."

"We've gotta run." Violet was shaking.

When the knob rattled again, Henry jumped back, colliding with Violet and Jessie. Benny crashed into Vita, knocking the camera out of her hands. It skidded across the floor and hit a wall at the far end of the living room.

In the middle of the wall was a door that the children hadn't noticed during their quick look around. The door was covered with the same peeling wallpaper as the rest of the room. Had it not been for a small latch and the gap near the floor, the door would have completely blended into the wall.

"Whoa," Vita said, scooping up her

seen left at the LaFonte mausoleum was in this closet. And there was plenty of room for today's final offerings.

"That's where my presents will go." Benny pointed to a big empty shelf near the back.

Henry turned toward Marcus. "You have a black coat like the one we saw in the cemetery. You were inside the café when the lily showed up. We saw you at the mausoleum. And we found the gifts in your family house." He scratched his forehead and ran a hand through his hair. "Everything seems to tell us that you are the thief. But I don't understand. Why would you steal your own candlesticks?"

"I promise you I didn't take my own candles," Marcus insisted. He looked over Henry's shoulder. "I've been to this old house a few times since I moved to town but never noticed that closet."

"It was hidden," Vita said. She shut the door to show him how the wallpaper perfectly matched up, making the door disappear into the wall.

"If you aren't the one pretending to be the ghost," Jessie said, opening her notebook and looking at Marcus's name on the suspect's page. "Who do you think it is?"

Vita was busy filming everything. She turned her camera to face the suspect. "What do you have to say, Mr. Michelson?"

"I don't—"

"Wait a second." Benny peered into Marcus's face. "Did you steal our dog?"

"I'm not the LaFonte ghost," Marcus said honestly. "But yes, I did take your dog."

CHAPTER 9

Who Is the Greenfield Ghost?

"You took our dog!" Benny stomped his feet. "That wasn't nice."

"I gave him water and food," Marcus assured Benny. "I did it because I wanted to get you out of the way." The college student looked from Benny to Jessie, to Violet and Henry. "I'm trying to find out who is pretending to be the ghost, and you children are always around, asking questions. You're ruining my investigation."

"We're searching for the same thing,"

Henry explained. "We could help each other."

"No," Marcus said. "I don't want help. I *need* to solve this mystery by myself."

"But we—" Henry began then changed his mind about what he was going to say. He looked to his siblings. "I just realized something important. Marcus is Madame LaFonte's grandson," Henry said.

"He is?" Violet asked. "How'd you know?"

"This is his family's house. He has the key," Henry explained. He asked Marcus, "You put out the candlesticks at the mausoleum so that you could see who took them, right?"

"Yes," Marcus said.

Jessie understood what had happened. She said, "When Mrs. Radcliffe said she chased someone else out of the cemetery that first night, it was Marcus. He was hiding to watch the candlesticks. Then, just like us, when he looked back from outside the cemetery—they were already gone."

"I missed seeing the thief and it's your fault. If I'd been the only one in the cemetery, Mrs. Radcliffe wouldn't have been so upset!" Marcus said, "I have to find out who ruined my family name. I want to prove there is no bad luck. And I have to do it on my own."

"But we're good helpers—" Violet began.

"No!" Marcus growled at her. "I'm close to finding the truth. If you kids mess this up, I'll have to wait another year until Jacqueline LaFonte's next anniversary. I need to find out who started the rumor so that my parents and cousins can move back to town. I want to rebuild this house, open a business again, and start a fresh life here." He turned to Henry. "Please stop getting in my way. Let me find the thief."

"How do you know your grandmother is not really a ghost?" Benny asked.

"Grandmother LaFonte would never have stolen gifts. She was a kind and charitable person," Marcus said. "Did you know she gave money to the children's hospital?

"Did she give money to families with sick children too?" Jessie asked. She drew her eyebrows together as the answer became clear.

"Yes," Marcus said. "How'd you know?"

"Oh," Henry said, putting a hand on Jessie's shoulder. "I'm pretty sure that we just figured out who the ghost is. There's someone living in Greenfield today who gives money and volunteers at the children's hospital, just like your grandmother did."

"I get it!" Benny said. "I know who the ghost is."

"Who?" Violet sneezed. "I'm not sure who you are talking about." She sneezed again.

"Violet's cold is a clue too," Benny said. "The ghost also has a cold."

"I got the cold the first night—" Violet's eyes grew wide as she realized what Benny had figured out. "Whew. I'm glad there's no real ghost." Violet whispered the answer to Vita.

"Who is it?" Marcus Michelson asked, following the children outside. "I'm sorry," he apologized. "I've treated you all badly. I was wrong."

"You need to apologize to Watch," Benny said. "You dog-napped him."

Marcus got down on one knee to pet Watch on the head. "Sorry, boy," he said. "I won't dog-nap any dog ever again."

Benny gave Marcus a long, hard look.

"Promise?"

"Promise," Marcus agreed. He stood up and faced the children. "You all are very good detectives and I made a mistake thinking I could solve this mystery on my own." He went on, saying, "I really do need your help."

"Miss Wolfson is pretending she's the LaFonte ghost," Henry told him.

"I thought it might be her," Marcus said, thinking about it. "She has a black coat. And she knows a lot about the ghost and has been encouraging people to bring gifts to the mausoleum."

"She was also in the café when the flower appeared," Violet said.

"And her coat was wet," Jessie reminded everyone.

"When Violet sneezed, I remembered that Miss Wolfson also has a cold," Benny said. "I think that they both got sick being in the cemetery late at night in the rain."

"It seems possible, but Miss Wolfson couldn't have been the ghost for the last seventy-four years," Marcus said. "No way. She's not old enough."

"That is a problem," Violet admitted.

"Miss Wolfson is the ghost now..." Henry said.

"But," Jessie finished Henry's thought, "maybe she wasn't the original LaFonte ghost."

CHAPTER 10

Trick or Treat

Mrs. Arlene Wolfson was sitting in a rocking chair near the front window of the nursing home's recreation center. She was alone, knitting a purple scarf. Her gray hair shone in the sunlight and she had a smile on her face.

"Visitors!" Mrs. Wolfson exclaimed. Her smile broadened as the Aldens, Marcus, and Vita entered the room. "I love visitors."

"Hi," Benny said. He walked directly to her and asked, "Were you the first LaFonte ghost?"

Mrs. Wolfson nodded. "So, you found me out." She winked and dropped her voice to a whisper. "I'm ninety-five years old, you know. For a very long time I've hoped someone would figure it out. But no one ever came to see me." She rocked back and forth in her chair.

"I remembered that your daughter, Miss Wolfson, volunteers at the children's hospital," Jessie said. "And gives money to families with sick children."

"So did my grandmother," Marcus said, introducing himself.

"It looks like you've carried on with Jacqueline LaFonte's work," Violet said to Mrs. Wolfson.

"Yes. Yes. The hospital was important to Jacqueline. We've given a lot of money in her honor over the last seventy-four years," Mrs. Wolfson said, still knitting. "Every year, I collected the gifts and then sold them. Every cent went to charity. I also donated any food gifts and flowers to people who really needed them." She raised her head and looked at the children. "When I got too old, my daughter took over the job."

"I think what you've done is nice," Violet said. "But taking gifts from others is stealing." She frowned. "You're kind of a generous thief."

"I know," Mrs. Wolfson replied, clicking her tongue and shaking her head. "That's the part that I feel terrible about. I never wanted to steal from anyone. Really. It's strange how it all worked out. I never meant for this to happen."

"How did it begin?" Marcus wanted to

know. "I've spent my whole life wondering why people here are afraid of my family."

"I'm very sorry about that. Everything got out of control too quickly. The rumors spread like fire. No matter how hard I tried, I couldn't stop the flames." Mrs. Wolfson told the children to bring chairs over from a nearby table. "Let me tell you a story."

After asking for permission, Vita turned on her camera.

"It started as a joke," Mrs. Wolfson said. "After Jacqueline LaFonte died, we thought it would be funny to play a Halloween prank on the town. A little trick. Everyone used to do Halloween tricks back then. Much more fun than getting treats." She told Marcus, "Your grandmother had such a great sense of humor. She'd passed away the year before, but still, we thought she'd love to be part of the prank."

Marcus gave a small smile. "Yes. My mother told me how Grandma LaFonte used to play practical jokes on everyone. Once she put a live turtle in my mom's bathtub. Another time she replaced all the flowers in the house with fake ones. Silly little things like that."

Mrs. Wolfson laughed. "Once, at the dress shop, she sewed a man's trouser legs together. He fell over when he tried to put them on. We laughed about it for days!"

"What did you do for the Halloween prank?" Violet asked.

"On the anniversary of her death, we put the lilies on her mausoleum, then set one in a shop in town. Patty made a big show of screaming in horror. She told everyone that before she died, Jacqueline said that anyone who didn't bring a present to her grave would have bad luck.

"The bad luck part was my idea," Mrs. Wolfson snickered. "It was very funny at first. Everyone was in a panic. Even people who didn't believe in ghosts or bad luck were bringing gifts—just in case." Her eyes clouded as she went on. "Patty and I thought it was the best joke ever played in Greenfield history. Better than when those boys put a cow in the mayor's office! Or the kids who dumped bubbles in the Main Street fountain." In a soft voice, she added, "We planned to give all the gifts back at the end of the three days."

"But Patty left town before it was over." Jessie knew that part of the story.

"Her sister got sick and needed help with her children. It was an emergency. Patty took the train the same day she heard the news." Mrs. Wolfson sighed. "Someone started a rumor that Patty had forgotten to leave a gift and disappeared." Her old shoulders sank. "Patty wrote me a letter that she wasn't coming back. Her sister needed her to stay. So, on my own, I went out to give back the gifts, but no one wanted them. They told me the ghost would harm them if they took back their presents."

Mrs. Wolfson stared out the window. "I tried and tried to explain. I talked until my voice hurt. No one wanted their things back. Finally, I gave up and donated the gifts to the hospital. I figured that Jacqueline would have liked hat."

"What happened next?" Marcus wanted to hear more.

"The following year, I didn't say anything about the ghost. No jokes. No pranks. No flowers. Nothing." Mrs. Wolfson raised her hands. "I couldn't believe it! The gifts piled up anyway." She shrugged. "I didn't know what to do. Again, I tried to give things back, but no one would take them. So once more, I donated them all."

"People started thinking my family brought bad luck." Marcus bit his bottom lip.

"It was bizarre. If a kid got the measles, they said it was the ghost. A dog got fleas. A man tripped on a curb…" Mrs. Wolfson said. "All anyone could talk about was the ghost's bad luck."

Violet let out a breath. She'd been holding it during the whole story. "This is terrible," she said. "Rumors can be very bad."

"After a few years, the LaFonte family moved away, and still the gifts kept coming on Jacqueline's anniversary. So I kept collecting them. I put them in the old empty house until I could send them to the hospital or sell them for money to give to families who needed it."

Vita moved in for a tight shot of Mrs. Wolfson's face.

"When I moved here to the nursing home, my daughter took over." She glanced out the window. Henry could see the cemetery in the distance.

"You made something good come from something bad," Violet said. "You're not really a thief, are you?"

Mrs. Wolfson hesitated as she considered how to answer. "I don't know. Yes. No. Sort of—"

The door to the room opened. "Hello," Miss Wolfson greeted her mother's visitors as she stepped inside. "Did Mom tell you the truth?" she asked the Aldens.

"Yes," Jessie said. "It's a crazy story."

"I know!" Miss Wolfson took off her jacket and threw it over the back of an empty chair. "I'm so glad you children believe there's no ghost," she said. "I wish we could convince the rest of the town."

"There must be something we can do," Jessie said.

"Let's just tell people the history," Marcus said. "After we share the truth, my family will move back to Greenfield. It'll be over."

"It's not that easy," Violet told him. "Remember when Jessie brought proof that

Patty Wilson didn't disappear because of the ghost's bad luck? She told everyone standing by the grave that Patty lived a long time. No one believed her."

"Just like no believed me all those years ago," Mrs. Wolfson said. "I'd have ended it seventy-four years ago if I could have."

"Well," Henry said, "we are going to have to *make* them believe us. No more bad luck. No more gifts."

Jessie thought about the words Mrs. Wolfson had used and said, "It's time to finally put out this fire."

"I definitely want the ghost story to end, but please don't forget about the hospital." Mrs. Wolfson was concerned. "The money, the flowers, and the food go to people who need it."

"Hmm," Marcus said. "That does make things complicated."

Vita lowered her camera. "Maybe..." she began. She turned the camera so that Henry could watch her whole movie from the beginning. "We can have a charity event for the hospital and get rid of the ghost at the same time."

"Leave it to us," Henry assured Miss Wolfson, Mrs. Wolfson, and Marcus. "We'll take care of everything!"

CHAPTER 11

Ghosts Gone?

The first annual Greenfield Halloween Charity Carnival took place in the cemetery parking lot.

"I knew there wasn't a real ghost," Benny said surely. "I knew it all along." He was standing in line for the Ferris wheel with Violet.

"So why are your pockets stuffed with granola bars?" Violet asked.

"In case I get hungry, of course," Benny said. He grinned and whispered, "Or in case we run into Mrs. Radcliffe. She still scares me." He shivered.

When Henry and Jessie went to the cemetery office to explain about the LaFonte ghost, they'd asked Mrs. Radcliffe if they could have the charity benefit in the cemetery.

"People are used to bringing gifts here," Henry had told her. "We simply want to take away the scary ghost part. They can donate whatever they want to the hospital."

Then Grandfather called Mrs. Wolfson at the nursing home and the younger Miss Wolfson at the historical society. He called the hospital to tell them about the charity carnival, and he called all his friends to come help.

Mrs. Wolfson and Miss Wolfson had set up the Greenfield Historical Society booth by the path to the cemetery. They entertained visitors with stories about Halloween pranks from Greenfield's town history.

From the top of the Ferris wheel, Benny could see that the place was packed. There were booths for games, a few fun rides, and in the center of it all stood the Children's Hospital LaFonte Donation Table.

"Bring your gifts here!" Jessie called out through a megaphone. There was a crowd of adults and children surrounding her. One by one, Jessie handed the gifts to Henry, who stood behind her.

"Drop off your donations to the children's hospital," Henry announced. He was piling the presents on a table.

Grandfather and Marcus Michelson were also standing at the table, wrapping the gifts in colored paper.

"Did you meet Marcus's mother?" Violet asked Benny as their swinging chair looped over the top of the wheel and began to sink back to earth.

"She's very nice," Benny said. "She makes dresses just like her mom did."

"I know!" Violet said. "She promised to make me something special. I can't wait. I picked out the fabric already. It's going to be purple to match the scarf Mrs. Wolfson made for me." She tightened the knitted scarf around her neck.

"I'm so glad we solved this mystery," Violet said as the owner of the café opened the gate

and let her and Benny off the ride. "It worked out for everyone. The rumors have stopped. The hospital gets presents. The LaFonte family can move back to town."

"Vita is showing her movie," Benny said. He checked the time. "We better hurry."

At the back of the parking lot a big white tent had been set up. The tent had long flaps to keep it dark inside.

Benny and Violet rushed to the front entrance.

"We're here," Violet told Vita.

"Just in time." Vita pointed to the line of people who'd come to see the movie. She told Violet where to stand. "Your job is to sell tickets. They cost a dollar. All the money will go to families with sick children."

Violet picked up a roll of tickets to sell. She was surprised when people gave her five or ten dollar bills and told her to keep the change.

"It's for charity," a woman said.

"It's good luck to give money to a good cause," a man said with a wink.

"Thanks!" Violet said, putting the money away and welcoming them into the tent.

Vita walked with Benny to another spot. "This is where you'll hand out popcorn," she told him. Smiling she added, "The popcorn was donated. It's free."

"Free food! My favorite kind." Benny stuffed a handful into his mouth.

"Save some for us, Benny," Henry said. He and Jessie entered the tent with Marcus and Grandfather. Behind them, the Wolfsons had also come to see the film.

"I hear I am going to be a celebrity," Mrs. Wolfson said.

"You sure are." A tall woman wearing a beautiful green suit stepped up to the group. "I'm Leanne Phuong. I came all the way from Hollywood to see Vita's movie. I'm a producer of ghost shows."

"You know there wasn't really ever a ghost," Miss Wolfson said, taking a bag of popcorn from Benny. "It was my mom. Then me."

"We know," Ms. Phuong assured her. "And we think it's a fabulous twist! A ghost story without a ghost. We are going to show this movie in film festivals all over the country."

Vita beamed. "Will you give all the ticket

sales to local hospitals?" Vita asked. "That's an important part of the story."

"Of course!" Ms. Phuong agreed.

"My first movie." Vita was very happy.

"You better get started on a second film project," Henry told her.

"I've been thinking I'll make that one about the historical society next," Vita said. "The one I started before all this happened. There's a lot of history in Greenfield." She waved her hand outside the tent toward Main Street.

"Ohhh!" Benny was so excited he nearly dropped a bag of popcorn. "Please, Vita," he said. "I want to be the star of your movie!"

Everyone laughed.

The Aldens sat together in the front row of the tent theater. Suddenly, the lights flickered and went off.

"Oh no," Benny said, jumping up from his chair. "Could there be another ghost in the cemetery? Yikes." He took a granola bar out of his pocket and began to unwrap it. "Maybe this time it's a zombie! Double yikes."

Jessie put a hand on Benny's shoulder.

"No ghost. No zombie. Not even a vampire. That was just Vita turning off the lights. The movie is starting."

A single lily sitting on a windowsill appeared on the screen.

"I don't believe in ghosts," Benny said firmly. Then he sat back to watch the movie.

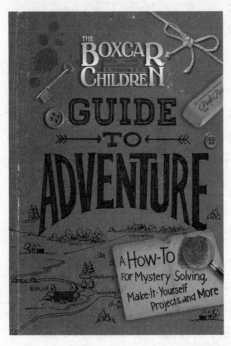

THE BOXCAR CHILDREN®

Fan Club

Join the Boxcar Fan Club!

Visit **boxcarchildren.com** and receive a free goodie
bag when you sign up. You'll receive occasional
newsletters and be eligible to win prizes
and more! Sign up today!

Don't Forget!

The Boxcar Children audiobooks are also available!
Find them at your local bookstore, or visit
oasisaudio.com for more information.

The adventures continue in the newest mysteries!

THE
BOXCAR
CHILDREN
THE MYSTERY OF THE MISSING POP IDOL

Created by
GERTRUDE CHANDLER WARNER

PB ISBN: 9780807556061, $5.99

THE BOXCAR CHILDREN

THE MYSTERY OF THE STOLEN DINOSAUR BONES

Created by
GERTRUDE CHANDLER WARNER

PB ISBN: 9780807556085, $5.99

THE BOXCAR CHILDREN

THE MYSTERY AT THE CALGARY STAMPEDE

Created by
GERTRUDE CHANDLER WARNER

PB ISBN: 9780807528419, $5.99

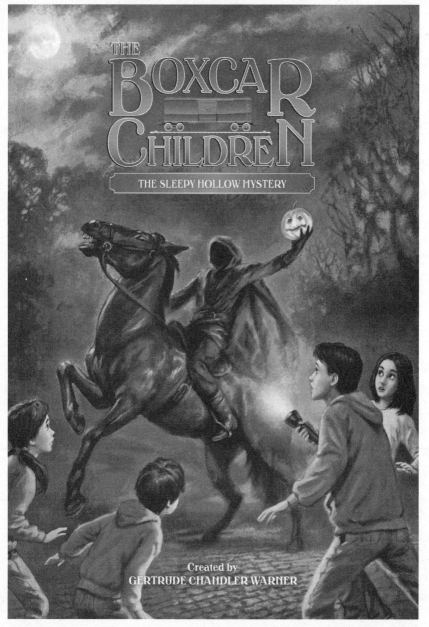

Downtown, they found crowds of people. "I smell something good," Benny said as they walked through the festival.

"The Apple House Café has a booth here," Annika told him. "You're smelling their apple custard tarts. They're famous for that."

Everyone tried the tarts.

"These are delicious." Jessie nibbled on hers slowly, tasting each bite. "I want to learn to make these too."

"Mr. Beekman is too mean to give you the recipe," Annika said. "I'll ask my mother if she knows how to make them. We should go say hello to Isiah. He's working in the library booth."

"That booth that says *library*," Benny said. "I see a girl dressed as an elf, but not Isiah."

Annika greeted the girl and asked, "Isn't Isiah supposed to be working?"

The girl slammed down a box of bookmarks. "Yes, but he didn't show up. I can't believe he didn't even call."

"He's been doing that too often," Annika said. "If I see him, I'll remind him he's supposed to be working. We should go. It's almost time for the parade."

"Look at those funny costumes." Benny pointed to some adults dressed as zoo animals walking by the booth. They were all carrying musical instruments.

"That's the band that leads the parade," Annika said. "We can follow them to the starting point. I wonder where Margot is. I thought she'd be here taking pictures. "

All the children and pets participating in the parade gathered at one end of the street. The band struck up a tune. The children began to march as the bystanders clapped for them.

They were halfway down the block when Violet stopped. "There's the headless horseman." She pointed up the street where a figure wearing a big black cape sat on a large black horse. It looked like there was no head above the cape.

"Maybe it's part of the parade," Henry suggested. "They could have someone dress up in costume to make the end of the parade more exciting."

"There's something strange about the horse," Jessie said. "It has red all around its eyes and mouth. And the coat is too shimmery for a normal horse."

Other children around them began to point as the horse and rider came closer. "That horse is scary," a little girl dressed as a fairy said.

Watch growled.

The horse reared up and gave an angry neigh.

GERTRUDE CHANDLER WARNER discovered when she was teaching that many readers who like an exciting story could find no books that were both easy and fun to read. She decided to try to meet this need, and her first book, *The Boxcar Children*, quickly proved she had succeeded.

Miss Warner drew on her own experiences to write the mystery. As a child she spent hours watching trains go by on the tracks opposite her family home. She often dreamed about what it would be like to set up housekeeping in a caboose or freight car—the situation the Alden children find themselves in.

While the mystery element is central to each of Miss Warner's books, she never thought of them as strictly juvenile mysteries. She liked to stress the Aldens' independence and resourcefulness and their solid New England devotion to using up and making do. The Aldens go about most of their adventures with as little adult supervision as possible—something else that delights young readers.

Miss Warner lived in Putnam, Connecticut, until her death in 1979. During her lifetime, she received hundreds of letters from girls and boys telling her how much they liked her books.